MURDER AT THE PONTE VECCHIO

T. A. WILLIAMS

Boldwood

First published in Great Britain in 2025 by Boldwood Books Ltd.

Copyright © T. A. Williams, 2025

Cover Design by JD Design Ltd.

Cover Images: Shutterstock

The moral right of T. A. Williams to be identified as the author of this work has been asserted in accordance with the Copyright, Designs and Patents Act 1988.

All rights reserved. No part of this book may be reproduced in any form or by any electronic or mechanical means, including information storage and retrieval systems, without written permission from the author, except for the use of brief quotations in a book review. This book is a work of fiction and, except in the case of historical fact, any resemblance to actual persons, living or dead, is purely coincidental.

Every effort has been made to obtain the necessary permissions with reference to copyright material, both illustrative and quoted. We apologise for any omissions in this respect and will be pleased to make the appropriate acknowledgements in any future edition.

A CIP catalogue record for this book is available from the British Library.

Paperback ISBN 978-1-83518-792-0

Large Print ISBN 978-1-83518-793-7

Hardback ISBN 978-1-83518-791-3

Ebook ISBN 978-1-83518-794-4

Kindle ISBN 978-1-83518-795-1

Audio CD ISBN 978-1-83518-786-9

MP3 CD ISBN 978-1-83518-787-6

Digital audio download ISBN 978-1-83518-789-0

This book is printed on certified sustainable paper. Boldwood Books is dedicated to putting sustainability at the heart of our business. For more information please visit https://www.boldwoodbooks.com/about-us/sustainability/

Boldwood Books Ltd, 23 Bowerdean Street, London, SW6 3TN

www.boldwoodbooks.com

To Mariangela and Christina with love as always

1

FRIDAY AFTERNOON

In a city as cosmopolitan as Florence, you see all sorts. Of course, there are the usual groups of tourists from all over the globe being herded about by guides waving flags, some even carrying their own microphones and loudspeakers, but sometimes you see some quite unique sights – and I'm not just referring to the Duomo or the statue of David.

Since setting up Dan Armstrong Private Investigations here in the city almost two years ago, I've got used to seeing people in medieval dress parading through the streets, tractors and trailers loaded with manure heading for the local government offices to complain about something or other, regular groups of protestors carrying banners advocating everything from saving the whales to legalising cannabis, and even a cortege of a hundred or so naked cyclists one freezing cold morning, but today was a first. As I made my way from my office to Anna's apartment just on the other side of the River Arno, I suddenly found myself confronted by a group of tigers – or should that be a pride or a pack?

I hasten to explain that these were not real members of the

big-cat family, but humans dressed up as tigers. The month of April had been particularly mild so far and the temperature showing on the illuminated sign above the entrance to a chemist's shop a hundred yards ahead of me was currently 21° – that's equivalent to a nice summer's day back in England. The people inside the stripy costumes must have been sweating buckets. Although I was slightly taken aback by this feline vision, Oscar appeared to take it in his stride. Had they been real cats – the domestic variety at least – he would have erupted into manic barking and set about chasing them from his territory, but all he did was stop and stare and, as one of the tigers approached, his tail started to wag. It wagged even harder when the tiger crouched down beside him and made a fuss of him.

'Who's a good boy? What a lovely dog.' It was a woman, speaking in English, and from her accent, she was Scottish. My Labrador is a very good listener, but I felt I should answer on his behalf.

'This is Oscar. I'm sure he's very pleased to meet you.'

The woman stood up and I saw her face peeking out at me beneath the tiger's slightly comical face with its big staring eyes and whiskers. 'Hi, I'm Amy. Are you English?'

From what I could see of her, she was probably in her mid-forties and from the colour of her cheeks, she was feeling the heat.

'Yes, I am, but I live here now.'

She beamed at me. 'You lucky man. Florence is so beautiful and so wonderfully historic, isn't it?'

I nodded in agreement. 'It certainly is. I have to ask: do you always go around dressed like this or is there a specific reason?'

'Lorraine's getting married.' She glanced sideways towards the rest of her group and lowered her voice. 'For the third time. We're all beginning to think she only does it for the hen parties.'

'So that's what this is: a hen party. But why the tiger costumes?'

'That was Lorraine's idea – she wanted cougar costumes but we couldn't find any, so tigers were the next best thing. It could have been worse – her original idea was harem girls.'

'I thought hen parties tended to take place in Magaluf or Ibiza or the like. What brought you to Florence?'

'It was my idea. I'm a lecturer in medieval and Renaissance history at Edinburgh University and I thought the girls would appreciate a bit of culture for a change. To be honest, the last time Lorraine got married, we all went to Marbella and it was pretty gross.'

'That's a coincidence – your subject, not Marbella. My partner lectures in medieval and Renaissance history here in Florence.' Anna and I had been together now for a year and a half, and living together since last summer, so I no longer referred to her as my girlfriend. 'Partner' seemed appropriate until we took the next step – if, indeed, we were to go down that route.

An expression of astonishment immediately appeared on the tiger's face.

'Do you mean Anna Galardo?' I nodded and she held out a stripy paw towards me. 'Dr Amy Mackintosh. I've known Anna for years, ever since she used to work at Bristol University. I was thinking about looking her up while I'm here, but I don't have a phone number for her.'

I shook her hand, wondering what I should do. Amy Mackintosh looked like a nice person but I thought it wiser to check with Anna before handing over her phone number, so I made a note of the Scottish tiger's phone number and promised I would get Anna to call. By coincidence, I was hosting a party this evening and one more guest wouldn't matter – although a dozen tigers might upset the balance a bit.

Tonight's event was being thrown by my new Italian publisher to celebrate publication of the Italian version of the first of my murder mysteries set here in Tuscany, and I had decidedly mixed feelings about it. Although I'd spent thirty years of my life in the Metropolitan Police, my hobby had always been writing, and now that I'd moved to Italy, I'd finally been lucky enough to achieve my ambition of becoming a published author. The book had come out in English a year earlier and was still continuing to sell pretty well, as did book number two, which had come out just before Christmas. As far as tonight was concerned, they had told me that all I had to do was turn up, shake a few hands, say a few words, read a couple of pages from the book and sign some copies for guests, but I wasn't looking forward to it. I'd invited some of the friends that I'd made since moving here two years ago, and the publisher had invited an unspecified number of local dignitaries, business people, academics, and even a few minor celebrities, but whether any of them would turn up was another matter.

I bade farewell to the stripy medievalist and headed back to Anna's place. I still thought of it as her place although I had spent most of the last six months living here. My own little house out in the country to the south of Florence came into its own in the hot summer months and at the weekends, but there was no getting away from the convenience of living only a fifteen-minute walk from the office. Private investigation business over the winter had been brisk, mainly the usual mix of unfaithful spouses, pilfering employees, and missing persons – with occasional exceptions.

Prime among these had been a mysterious creature invading a poultry farm to the east of the city and attacking its avian inhabitants. I had set up a series of surveillance cameras, with the aid of which the perpetrator had been revealed as a neighbour's cat called Napoleon. The cat might even make it into one of my books some time but, although I still enjoyed my writing, I was struggling to find the time. Ideas for new whodunnits continued to flash through my mind all the time, and as I walked back past Piazza della Repubblica, I wondered idly whether a group of Brits dressed in tiger costumes might form the nucleus of a convincing plot. Anything was possible.

When I got to the Ponte Vecchio, I paused in the centre of the bridge and looked around. Even though Easter weekend had come and gone, it was still crowded with tourists. I looked out over the muddy waters of the River Arno, marvelling as always at how the level of the river could possibly have risen by ten metres or more during the catastrophic floods of 1966. Now, even though winter had only just finished, the water level was still unusually low, and I hoped the predictions of drought wouldn't come true. My house in the country was set among olive groves and vineyards, and I knew that last year, the local farmers had really struggled with what had been one of the hottest and driest summers on record. As I was an Englishman, it felt totally alien to be hoping for rain, but I knew that this was what was needed.

The Ponte Vecchio, the 'Old Bridge', was built in medieval times and it has the distinction of being a bridge lined with shops. These tiny boutiques flanking both sides of the bridge – many actually sticking out over the sides – are now predominantly jewellers, although Anna had told me that back when the bridge was first constructed, they had mainly been butchers' shops and the stench had been unbearable. Nowadays, it's far more civilised but, as a World Heritage site, it draws millions of visitors every year and, for those of us just interested in getting from one side of the river to the other, it could be a real pain having to weave through the mass of humanity milling about there. The Medici family, Florence's most famous ruling dynasty, had foreseen this problem and ordered the construction of the

Vasari Corridor – a private covered walkway built over the heads
of the populace so they could get from their home in Palazzo Pitti
to their place of work at the Palazzo Vecchio and back undis-
turbed. I often wish they'd given me the keys.

Anna's apartment is on the second floor of a sixteenth-century
building less than a hundred metres from the bridge, and I found
her with the ironing board set up in the middle of the living
room. As Oscar trotted across to greet her, I realised that the
garment she was ironing was none other than my new, very
expensive suit. When I lived in the UK, I only ever used to buy
most of my clothes from Marks & Spencer or the like, but since
being partnered with an Italian, all that had changed. Determined that I should look my best for tonight's party, Anna had
marched me into town a week ago and had chosen an admittedly
very smart, dark-grey suit for me, but when I'd seen the price, I
had come close to making a run for it. Still, I'd told myself, it
probably was time for a new suit, although the opportunities to
wear it here were scarce. Work clothes for me nowadays were
definitely casual. After years of collars and ties at Scotland Yard,
the change had been liberating. Tonight, on the other hand,
promised to be much more formal.

'*Ciao, bella*. Thanks for ironing the suit, but surely it didn't
need it. I haven't worn it yet.' After her being married to an
Englishman for twenty years and having lived in the UK, Anna's
English is better than my Italian, so we normally speak English
together. This afternoon, she answered me in Italian and I knew
her well enough by now to realise that this meant that she was
feeling stressed.

'You're back at last! You said you'd be home at three. Do you
realise we have to be at the restaurant in less than two hours'
time?'

I checked my watch and saw that it was just after four. As far as I was concerned, that was plenty of time to get ready, but I didn't say that to her. Instead, I headed for the kitchen and answered in Italian.

'How does a cup of tea sound?'

Oscar followed me into the kitchen, where his nose immediately pointed at the cupboard where his biscuits lived.

Anna's voice followed me. 'Yes, please, but don't make it too strong.'

After years of the Scotland Yard canteen, I'd grown used to tea strong enough to take the enamel off your teeth, but since meeting Anna, I'd had to change my ways. I made a mug of weak tea for her and a mug of slightly stronger tea for me, gave Oscar one of his bone-shaped biscuits and headed back into the living room. As I did so, I remembered the tigers.

'As I was walking here I met somebody who knows you. Does the name Dr Amy Mackintosh mean anything to you?'

Anna looked up from her ironing and her expression was hard to read. On the one hand, there was surprise and pleasure, but on the other was something else, and I struggled to identify it. As somebody who had spent his working life trying to analyse people's reactions, this was a tricky one. It took me a few moments before I thought I'd managed to narrow it down to a mixture of embarrassment and pain. Why, I wondered, might that be?

I listened with interest as Anna responded. 'Amy? Well, well, well, I've known her for years. She teaches in Edinburgh. What's she doing in Florence?'

I told her about the tiger costumes and Anna's expression lightened – a little, but there was still that discomfort. My curiosity increased, but I thought it best to let Anna tell me all about it in due course – rather than now when she was already a bit stressed. I was pleased to see her reach for her phone so, whatever it was that was troubling her, it hadn't stopped her from speaking to the Scot.

'Give me her number and I'll give her a call. Shall I ask her to come tonight?'

'If it's okay with you, it's okay with me so go ahead and invite her. By all means.' She made the call and a five-minute conversation ensued, during which I was relieved to hear her sounding fairly normal and not strained. I was also pleased to hear her suggest that the tiger costume might not be quite what was wanted for tonight's event. I sat back on the sofa and did my best to stop wondering what might have been behind Anna's unexpected reaction at hearing Amy's name. I took refuge in fiction and, as so often, I let my imagination take over and I was already envisaging a tiger-clad academic floating face down in a fountain and another escaping from the police down the autostrada at ninety miles an hour when Anna's call ended and she came over to sit beside me, rousing me from my musings.

'Right, she's coming.' That strange, uncertain look was still on her face, but I saw her make an effort and return to the more pressing matter of what I was going to be doing this evening. 'Now, do you want to go over your speech one more time?'

I didn't really, but it probably made sense to do as she said so I launched into it while she sat back and nodded approvingly. Her approval was probably less for my delivery than for the content, most of which she had been responsible for writing. Although I've done a fair bit of public speaking in my time, I've never been terribly keen on it – especially in a foreign language. I got to the end of it and looked over at her.

'Will that do? It doesn't come across as too boastful, does it? It's only a whodunnit, after all, not an acceptance speech for a Nobel prize.'

She reached over and gave my hand a reassuring squeeze. 'It'll be fine, Dan. I'm sure they'll love it.'

I hoped she was right, but it was too late now to pull out of it. Instead, I found myself wondering yet again why she had reacted the way she had. It promised to be an interesting evening in more ways than one.

2

FRIDAY EVENING

I'm not sure whether they loved it or not, but my little performance seemed to go down all right, and I got a round of applause at the end of it. As I delivered my speech, I looked around the room and was pleasantly surprised to see so many people. Among the guests I spotted some of my closest friends here in Italy, notably Commissario Virgilio Pisano of the Florence murder squad and his right-hand man, Inspector Marco Innocenti. Along with them was Virgilio's wife, Lina, who now worked for me as my PA, receptionist, secretary, and occasional dog walker. Beyond them was a sea of faces of other people, most of whom I didn't recognise, although the smartly dressed gentleman sitting with the representatives of the publishing house in the middle of the front row looked familiar. It took me a while to work out that this was none other than the *sindaco*, Mr Mayor himself. How they had managed to get him to come to this very minor event was beyond me.

As soon as my speech ended, the managing director of the publishing company came up to congratulate me and to introduce me to the mayor. Like so many people in authority these days, the mayor was younger than me, probably by ten years or so, and he was a charming and affable character. It quickly emerged that he was also a writer – in his case of historical novels set here in the city – and his books were published by the same company. No doubt this explained his appearance here tonight and the presence of a couple of newspaper photographers, for whom the three of us posed with cheesy smiles on our faces – or at least on mine.

While waiters circulated with glasses of spumante and trays of nibbles, I spent the next hour or more answering questions from people, signing copies of my book, and generally doing my best to promote the new publication. It was almost eight before I managed to get back to Anna, who had found a table in a corner where she and Amy Mackintosh were sitting. I hadn't been present when Amy had arrived and I was relieved to see them sitting together now and chatting reassuringly normally, with Oscar sprawled at their feet. He looked up as he saw me appear, gave a lazy wag of the tail, and subsided into somnolence once more. Anna pushed out a chair for me and leant over to give me a kiss when I sat down.

'I told you it would all go well, didn't I?' She sounded triumphant – and certainly much more relaxed than earlier. 'Have you had a drink? You look as if you could do with one.'

I gave her a smile. 'I thought it best to stay off the booze, at least until I'd done my duty. I've hardly had a chance to speak to Virgilio or Marco or any of the others I invited. It's maybe just as well Tricia couldn't come. I doubt if I would have been able to spend more than a few minutes with her.' My daughter lived and worked in the UK and although she had indicated that she would have been keen to come to the event, her work as a solicitor had prevented her from getting away.

'What about food? Have you eaten?' Anna was sounding more

concerned. No sooner had she spoken than there was a movement at our feet and Oscar's face appeared by my right knee, doing his unsuccessful best to look as if he was in the latter stages of starvation. When it comes to food, his comprehension skills are unparalleled – in English or in Italian.

I shook my head and Anna jumped to her feet. 'Leave it to me.'

After she had disappeared into the slowly diminishing crowd, as people started to drift away, I looked across at Dr Mackintosh and saw her smile.

'I had no idea Anna had found herself a murder-mystery writer. How exciting!'

I smiled back. 'When I can find the time. I have a pretty full-on job, so the only time I can write is in the evenings if I'm lucky.'

'What do you do, if you don't mind me asking?'

'I have a private investigation agency here in Florence. I used to be in the Metropolitan Police murder squad until I retired a few years ago, so it seemed like a sensible new venture.'

'How exciting. I've never met a private eye before. What sort of thing do you do? Is it dangerous?'

I was quick to disabuse her. 'It's not like it is on the TV. I certainly don't carry a gun and I don't go around getting shot at – at least not so far. Most of my time's spent waiting around, spying on people – I'm afraid marital infidelity is what keeps me busiest – and, increasingly, computer fraud.' I nodded towards her wedding ring. 'What about your husband? Does he have an exciting job?'

She smiled. 'He's a geologist, and I'm afraid I can't get worked up about rocks the way he does. He's currently working on something to do with diamonds but, sadly, he doesn't bring any free samples home with him.'

I glanced around but there was no sign of Anna for the

moment so I allowed myself a few moments of being a detective. 'So, how do you know Anna, then?'

Now it was Amy's time to look awkward. 'We used to see each other at seminars and conferences, but it was only when we worked out that we had something other than history in common that we became friends.'

I caught her eye. 'And that was...?'

That same expression of embarrassment and pain I had noted on Anna's face appeared on her face now. 'We were both going through breakups, followed by divorce. She rapidly became my shoulder to cry on and I became hers.' She produced a wry smile. 'And we did a lot of crying.'

I gave her a sympathetic smile in return as it all became clear to me. 'Divorces are tough. You don't need to tell me. I've been through one myself.'

At that moment Anna returned with a tray. On it was a plate containing a selection of tiny sandwiches, mini bruschetta, and slices of salami on squares of grilled polenta. There were also two glasses of fizz and a large glass of cold beer. She set the tray down, handed me the beer, and took a seat.

'Here, Dan, I thought you might be desperate for something cold.'

I blew her a kiss. 'You know me so well.' I took a cool, refreshing mouthful and gave a happy sigh – partly fuelled by the drink, but more so by the explanation Amy had just given me. 'Ah, wonderful, I needed that. Now I can relax.'

We sat and chatted over our selection of snacks and drinks until, all too soon, I was summoned by the publishers once again to say goodbye to the important guests. I shook hands with a variety of people whose names I felt sure I would never remember, until it was the turn of the mayor. To my surprise, instead of shaking my hand, he took me by the arm and led me out of the door and into the street. I went with him, intrigued to see where this might be heading. Was he maybe going to warn me off the publishers? I certainly hoped not as I had already signed and sealed the deal with them. The sun had set and it was almost dark, but the street was still busy. When the mayor was sure that we weren't being overheard, he started to speak and I realised that what he had to say had nothing to do with books.

'I'm sorry it's taken me so long to put two and two together, but I realise now that you're the private investigator, aren't you?'

'That's what pays the bills. I used to be in the police in London and setting up as a PI seemed like a good idea.'

'A very good idea, I'm sure, and you have an excellent reputation. Your name was mentioned to me recently by my good friend, the *questore*. I gather you've helped out our local police on a few occasions.'

'I sometimes lend a hand if there are English speakers involved.' I found myself wondering just where he was going with this. The *questore* was roughly equivalent to a chief constable or the police commissioner in the UK, and somebody who wielded a lot of power. I had heard of him but had never met him. What, I wondered, had prompted such an august person to bring up my name?

A noisy group of tourists came walking past and the mayor waited until they were out of earshot before continuing. 'We can't talk here. I wonder if you could spare me a few minutes of your time early next week, maybe Monday or Tuesday. I'd like to ask your advice about something confidential. Could you do that?'

'Yes, of course, I'd be pleased to help in any way. When would suit you?'

'I'll have to check with my secretary, but maybe we could have lunch together. Would that be all right?'

I agreed immediately, fascinated at the thought of what he

might want to tell me, and we exchanged phone numbers before shaking hands. He congratulated me and wished me well with my book and I was quick to offer my good wishes for his writing in return. He headed off in the direction of the Ponte Vecchio and I went back into the function room, which was emptying rapidly.

My intention was to return to where Anna and Amy were sitting, but I found myself waylaid when an insistent hand caught my arm and I turned to see a wiry old man, quite possibly in his eighties, standing at my side. He had an unkempt mass of white hair and a bushy moustache, which gave him a slightly Einstein-like appearance, and the expression on his face was dead serious. I wondered what might be troubling this stranger so I gave him a welcoming smile.

'Good evening, have you been here for the book launch?'

He didn't respond to my smile. 'I didn't come for that, Signor Armstrong. I came because I'm interested in speaking to you in your professional capacity.'

I took my time before replying, my brain churning. What should have been an evening dedicated to my murder mysteries was throwing up mysteries of its own. First the mayor and his mysterious invitation to dine with him, and now this old man. I answered cautiously.

'How can I help you, Signor...?'

'Berg, David Berg. I have a jewellery shop on the Ponte Vecchio.' His Italian was faultless but I felt I could detect an unusual accent lurking there although I couldn't pinpoint it. His name sounded Germanic and I wondered if he was maybe from the German-speaking part of Italy, far to the north, near the border with Austria. As I studied him, I was struck by his hard face and remarkably cold eyes. Despite my initial impression of him, this was no charming old duffer. He might be old, but he looked as sharp as a tack and as tough as nails, and he certainly didn't radiate bonhomie.

I answered politely. 'And do you have a problem?'

He nodded again. 'I do indeed have a problem and I need the help of a professional such as yourself.'

'Is it a business problem or a personal problem?'

He paused before replying. 'A bit of both.' He stopped and waited as a pair of guests walked out past us and stopped to shake me by the hand and wish me well. Once they had left, he continued. 'We obviously can't speak here.' I suppressed a smile as he repeated almost the same words used by the mayor. 'It would be best if you come to my shop so I can outline the situation to you. The shop closes at seven-thirty in the evening so you should come at that time or just after, so I can talk freely.' Those hard eyes caught mine for a moment. This was a man who was used to getting his own way. 'Don't worry, I'm prepared to pay for your services. Bring your terms and conditions with you.'

I agreed and we arranged that I would come to his shop on Monday evening. We shook hands and I made my way back across the room to where Anna was still sitting. She looked up as I approached. 'You took your time. Everything all right? I saw you disappear out of the door with the mayor and I wondered if he was about to offer you the keys of the city.'

I smiled and shook my head. 'Chance would be a fine thing. No, we had a little chat.' I deliberately try to keep Anna separate from my work where possible to avoid bringing work problems home with me. That had to a great extent been the cause of my original divorce well over two years ago, so for now, I told her a little white lie. 'As we both now work for the same publishing house, we were just exchanging notes. The mayor seems like a pleasant chap and he's invited me for lunch one day next week. That's rather nice of him, isn't it?'

Anna nodded approvingly and Amy glanced at her watch. 'I'd better go. The girls were going out for dinner somewhere in the centre and then they said they were going clubbing. The last thing I feel like is a noisy disco, but I suppose I'd better go and keep an eye on them. They do have a tendency to get themselves into trouble. Thank you very much for inviting me to your soirée. It's been great to meet you, Dan, and to catch up with Anna. And, Dan, the first thing I'm going to do when I get back to the UK is to buy a copy of your book in English.'

She gave us both a kiss, hugged Oscar, and left in search of her hens. I glanced across at Anna and smiled at her. 'Amy told me you two were divorce buddies. There were times when I wished I'd had a shoulder to cry on when my marriage was falling apart.'

She smiled back, a genuine, happy smile. 'That's all behind us now, Dan. Amy has her new husband and that all sounds as if it's going well. As for me, I can't complain. I didn't just get a wonderful man; I got a sloppy Labrador into the bargain.'

Reassured that all was well with her – and me – I reached for the remains of my beer and settled back in my seat, wondering what my two brief encounters this evening were likely to bring. Was it just coincidence that the mayor of the city and a jeweller on the Ponte Vecchio both appeared keen to have the services of a private investigator? I looked forward to seeing how that worked out.

3

SATURDAY MORNING

Although it had rained in the night, it was a pleasant, sunny morning when I took Oscar for his early walk. There was still a bit of night-time chill in the air, but it looked like being another sparkling spring day. I turned right outside Anna's front door and headed back towards the Ponte Vecchio. My intention was to turn right again when we reached the bridge and head up the hill past the beautiful Pitti Palace away from the town centre so as to give Oscar a chance to stretch his legs without encountering crowds of tourists. However, when we got to the bridge, my attention was drawn to a couple of police cars parked across the entrance to it, with a pair of police officers in uniform effectively blocking access to this major tourist attraction. Intrigued, I wandered over and was pleased to see a familiar face. It was my old friend Inspector Marco Innocenti. I had first met him when he'd been a sergeant and I'd always rated him as a very competent police officer.

'*Ciao*, Marco, what's got you out of bed at seven-thirty on a Saturday morning?' Oscar, spotting his old buddy, trotted over to greet him as the two of us shook hands.

'Some guy's decided to hang himself off the bridge.'

After thirty years in the murder squad, I was no stranger to violent death, but it came as a shock all the same. 'Here on the Ponte Vecchio? What a place to choose. Does it look suspicious?'

Marco shook his head. 'Doesn't appear so. No signs of a struggle.'

'Is Virgilio there? I didn't get a chance to talk to either of you last night. Thanks a lot for coming, by the way.'

He shook his head. 'The *commissario's* probably still in bed if he's got any sense. I saw no need to get him out for something as straightforward as this. Sergeant Dino is not due back from sick leave for another few weeks so I came myself. All right, the Ponte Vecchio isn't most people's first choice as a place to end it all but, when it's all said and done, from a police perspective, it's still pretty routine.' He gave me a cheeky grin and changed the subject. 'I thought your speech last night was great. Did you get lots of your fans giving you their phone numbers and throwing their underwear at you?'

I grinned back at him. 'No such luck, but I did get an invitation to lunch with the mayor.' A nudge of Oscar's nose against my leg reminded me of his priorities. 'Anyway, I'd better take Oscar for his walk. If you see Virgilio, tell him I'll give him a call later on.'

Florence is a frustrating city for dog owners. If you look down on it from above, there are numerous parks and open areas of green space, but so many of them are private and locked up behind high iron railings. The famous Boboli Gardens behind Palazzo Pitti are only five minutes from Anna's house but because they are categorised as an open-air museum, dogs aren't allowed in. As a result, over the winter months, I'd come up with a route along a series of narrow lanes leading up the hill to the south of Florence and back again where we wouldn't meet much traffic. Today, this would give us both some exercise before we headed out to my home in the country for the weekend where Oscar could run to his heart's content.

When we got back to the apartment, I found Anna already up and dressed, filling a basket with provisions for the next two days. Decamping to the country at the weekends had become a regular habit over the winter and as the warmer weather approached, it would soon be time to move out to Montevolpone permanently until the autumn brought us back into the city again. Not for the first time, I reflected on my good fortune. Being able to spend my life in such beautiful surroundings – whether in the city or in the hills – made me a very lucky man. Although I still loved much about England, I had to admit that Tuscany, with its historic beauty, its warm weather and, of course, its wonderful food and drink, took a lot of beating.

We set off in my VW minivan at just after nine and we were at my place by half past. The little house I'd bought over a year ago is situated partway up a hillside and access is up a fairly rough track dressed with chalky white gravel, one of Tuscany's famous *strade bianche* – the white roads. Anna told me she had stuff to do, so I put on a pair of shorts and took Oscar out for a proper walk. As I followed him uphill past olive groves and vineyards, throwing sticks and pine cones for him to retrieve, I thought back to the previous night.

My forthcoming meeting with the mayor promised to be interesting. I still couldn't imagine what the 'confidential' matter that he wanted to discuss with a random English private eye might be. I just hoped it wasn't political. Politics in Italy can be very confusing and everybody seems to have a strong opinion about one party or another – and there are over a dozen to choose from, all with different acronyms – so I've always tried to steer clear of the subject. Of course, it could well be a personal matter, and when we got to the top of the hill, I pulled out my phone and checked up on him.

Ugo Gallo was fifty-two years old – so almost six years younger than I was – and he had originally been an architect before becoming a politician. He had been married for twenty-three years and had twin daughters, both studying at Florence university. As far as I could see, his private life was unblemished, so it looked likely that the confidential matter would prove to be something else. I looked forward to finding out.

As for the elderly man with the jeweller's shop who had accosted me last night, I hoped I wasn't going to discover that he'd been the person who had chosen to take his own life on the Ponte Vecchio. He had certainly looked and sounded worried about something, but why would he make an appointment to see a private investigator and then kill himself only a few hours after making the appointment? This would make little sense and, besides, there had been that inner strength to the man that I had sensed. This, more than anything, made me feel it highly unlikely he would ever have contemplated suicide. Mind you, I told myself, whoever the victim was, he had chosen an iconic place to end it all.

It was a beautiful morning and Oscar and I walked for two solid hours, returning home shortly before midday feeling hot, sweaty and hungry. In Oscar's case, this was no surprise. He's always hungry. As for me, in spite of a plate of sandwiches the previous night followed by a *quattro stagioni* pizza, I had built up quite a hunger, and the first thing I did when I got home was to suggest to Anna that I would do a barbecue lunch. In the fridge, I had some particularly good pork sausages made by our local butcher and a massive Florentine T-bone steak the size of a King James Bible that could have fed a family of four.

With this in mind, Anna made a sensible suggestion: 'Why

don't I do pasta for lunch to keep you going, and we invite Virgilio and Lina for a barbecue tonight?'

I nodded in agreement and pulled out my phone. When Virgilio answered, his voice sounded a bit weary, and it took a bit of persuading to get him to agree to come out to our place for dinner that evening. Being a police officer is a full-on job and I knew from experience that Virgilio lived and breathed his work – just as I had done until my wife had left me and I'd taken early retirement in the vain hope of winning her back. As I put the phone down again, I found myself reflecting on his lacklustre tone and hoping that things were all right between him and Lina.

While Anna made pasta alla carbonara, I switched on the TV to get the forecast for the rest of the weekend and found that the mysterious death on the Ponte Vecchio had already reached the local media. The person who had been found hanging suspended from the middle of the bridge was described as being an elderly man, but the police had not yet revealed his name. This set me thinking. There were tens of thousands of elderly men in Florence and, indeed, before too long I would find myself joining their ranks, but it did strike me as a coincidence – and I've never liked coincidences. As I consumed my very good lunch, I couldn't help thinking about the old man who had approached me last night and, when the meal ended, I couldn't resist picking up my phone again and calling Inspector Marco Innocenti. As usual, he answered almost immediately.

'*Ciao*, Dan.'

'*Ciao*, Marco. Can I ask you something, just to satisfy my curiosity? The body found this morning hanging from the Ponte Vecchio, it wasn't by any chance a gentleman called David Berg, was it?'

'Yes, it was.' He sounded surprised. 'But how do you know

that? We're still trying to contact his next of kin and his identity hasn't been released yet.'

I felt a surge of surprise go through me at the thought that the old man I'd met only a few hours earlier had chosen to take his own life. This was immediately followed by an equally strong wave of scepticism. I did my best to explain to Marco the circumstances in which I'd met him, ending with the words, 'So why did he make an appointment to see me on Monday and then kill himself only a few hours after fixing it up? It makes no sense.'

When Marco answered, I could tell that he was as bewildered as I was. 'I agree. I'm still waiting for the pathologist's report, but his initial impression was that there were no signs of it being anything other than suicide. You said the guy was looking and sounding worried when he spoke to you. Do you think he might have allowed his worries to get on top of him that night and decided to end it all? Had he been drinking, do you think?'

'He certainly didn't sound drunk, and the spumante at my party wasn't the strongest wine on the planet. No, he just looked worried, but he also looked remarkably resilient. I find it hard to believe that he was the sort of man to take his own life.'

'And he gave no clue as to what it was that was worrying him?'

'No, not so much as a hint. I asked him if it was business or personal and he said, "a bit of both," but I've no idea what he meant. But surely, if he was contemplating hiring the services of a private investigator, it must have been something serious – at least serious to him – but what?'

Marco must have heard the frustration in my voice. 'Who knows? Well, let's see what Gianni says when he's finished the autopsy. I'll give you a call or send you a text when I hear something, okay?'

I thanked him, rang off, and spent the next few hours wondering what might be behind the old man's sudden death while I split some logs for the wood burner and pulled up a few weeds that were already appearing in the flower beds. It had been such a brief conversation the previous night and I knew next to nothing about the victim, so it was an almost impossible task to try to guess what might have been worrying him. I still found it hard to believe that the hard-faced, determined man I'd met should have chosen to take his own life. Of course, in the right circumstances, anybody can feel suicidal but, considering that I'd quite possibly been one of the last people to see him alive, I hadn't gained that impression from him at all.

At just after four o'clock, I was sitting outside under the loggia, the fresh green shoots on the vines and clematis serving to shelter me from the remarkably warm April sunshine. I had a mug of tea in my hand, my human partner at my side, and my four-legged canine partner sprawled at my feet. I felt remarkably relaxed and content, thanking whatever lucky stars there were that I'd made the decision to give up life in London and move over here. Bees were humming above me, the view down the hill over the wide valley of the River Arno towards the tree-clad Apennines in the far distance was as delightful as ever, and I felt at one with the world.

Then my phone rang. It was Marco.

'*Ciao*, Dan. It wasn't suicide after all. Gianni says the old guy died of a heart attack caused by manual strangulation before he was hung out to dry. There were clear thumb prints around his throat beneath the marks caused by the noose as well as signs of somebody assaulting or interrogating him. There were distinct bruises to his torso consistent with him taking a beating.'

'So he was already dead when somebody tied a noose around his neck and dumped him over the side of the bridge? That's macabre.'

'It truly is. Ever since Gianni called me, I've been trying to get my head around it. The way I see it, the old man must have been in the shop when his assailant arrived. The shop was closed, so why did the victim open the door to him? Did they know each other? The assault must have taken place inside the shop, out of sight of passers-by, in the course of which the old man died. Maybe the assailant went there with the intention of killing, or maybe he was trying to rob him, but accidentally went too far with his intimidating behaviour, and as a result, the old man dropped dead. The killer then found himself with the problem of what to do with the body. Should he leave it there to be found or should he try to make it look like suicide? As we know, he opted for the sham suicide, but he was taking a hell of a risk of being seen.'

'Did Gianni give a time of death?'

'This is where it gets interesting. Death occurred quite a few hours before the "hanging". Gianni says the victim was probably killed between eight and ten last night, but the fake hanging wasn't until around two o'clock in the morning.'

I hesitated while my brain processed the implications of what I'd just been told. 'It was probably around eight-fifteen or so when I last saw Berg, so, assuming he went straight back to his shop after speaking to me, his killer was quite possibly waiting for him and followed him inside. Any sign of forced entry?'

'No, although his shop and the little apartment above it had been ransacked. Forensics are in there at the moment, but it's a hell of a mess.'

'An apartment? Did he live on the bridge?'

'I doubt it. There's just a tiny one-room apartment above the shop, used as a storeroom.'

'Any idea what was taken, assuming it was robbery?'

'No idea at all. There was a lot of fairly cheap jewellery still lying about, but presumably, the thief removed the more valuable stuff.'

'Is there a safe there?'

'Yes. Forensics say it's an ancient model and should be easy enough for them to open. It has a pass combination rather than a key so maybe the killer was trying to get Berg to reveal the combination when the old boy's heart gave out.'

This sounded like the most likely scenario and I was quick to agree. 'I'm sure you're right that the murder was the work of a thief who killed the old man – deliberately or accidentally – while trying to get his hands on what was in the safe. When Berg dropped dead, he presumably helped himself to a bag full of jewellery as the next best thing. I wonder if Berg had anything of serious value in the safe. I bet the murderer was frustrated not to get access to it. With Berg dead, all he could do was sit by the dead body until the small hours when the bridge was deserted before setting up the phoney suicide attempt.'

'That's what it looks like. Poor old guy.'

* * *

Virgilio and Lina arrived just after six. Oscar gave a boisterous greeting to both of them and even managed to raise a smile on the *commissario's* face. Although the Italian police force has a more complex ranking system than the Metropolitan Police, *commissario* roughly equates to chief inspector, which made us both the same rank. This, apart from anything else, explained why we'd become close friends, and when I saw him this evening, I was immediately concerned at his appearance – I'd never seen him looking so troubled. I handed him a glass of red wine made by Fausto, the friendly farmer just over the hill from here, and did my best to get to the bottom of what might be bothering him, but without success. Virgilio remained remarkably taciturn, and even the prospect of some exceptionally good grilled meat didn't appear to cheer him. In the end, I decided that all I could do was to offer him my support, so I took him to one side as I was finishing grilling the last of the sausages and spoke quietly into his ear.

'If something's bothering you, you know I'm here, don't you? If I can help in any way, don't hesitate.'

He looked up from the hot coals and met my eye for a moment. 'Thanks, Dan, you're a good friend. Unfortunately, it's not the kind of thing I can talk about.'

At least, I thought to myself, he had admitted that he had something on his mind, but I was no closer to knowing what this might be. Lina appeared to be fairly normal, although I could see her casting concerned looks at her husband from time to time. No doubt she was aware that he was worried about something but, by the look of it, she was no closer than I was to knowing the reason.

Modestly speaking, it was a very good meal. The steak was excellent and I reckoned my barbecuing skills had developed sufficiently to do the meat justice. Anna had made a huge mixed salad containing everything from artichoke hearts to olives, quails' eggs to walnuts, and we finished the meal off with meringue ice cream from the local gelateria and some of last year's apricots from the garden that Anna had conserved in syrup. I deliberately didn't mention the death on the Ponte Vecchio as I had a feeling Virgilio's worries might turn out to be work-related and instead, I concentrated on cheering him up. For his part, he made no mention of police business at all, which only confirmed my supposition that something at work was playing on his mind.

By the time they left, he had at least had a smile on his face a few times, but he was still looking unusually sombre. This had not gone unnoticed by Anna, who turned to me as the tail lights of his car disappeared down the track.

'What's the matter with Virgilio?'

I shook my head. 'I wish I knew. There's definitely something wrong, but he won't say what it is.'

'Lina's worried. She told me he's been like it for days now and, just like with you, he refuses to tell her what's the matter. Isn't there any way you can sit down with him man-to-man and get him to talk? It saddens me to see him so troubled.'

It saddened me too. What, I wondered, had he meant when he'd said, 'It's not the kind of thing I can talk about'?

4

SUNDAY MORNING

Next morning, I received a call while I was out with Oscar for our early-morning walk. It was Marco.

'*Ciao*, Dan, sorry to bother you on a Sunday. Are you busy this morning?'

'Nothing special planned. Why, what's the problem?'

'It's the family of the victim. They don't speak Italian.'

'The old man sounded fluent to me, although he had a bit of an accent. What language do the relatives speak?'

'They're Dutch, but they claim to speak English. The victim was originally from the Netherlands, but he moved here thirty years ago after his wife divorced him, but his children – two boys and a girl – stayed in Amsterdam with the mother.'

'So do you want me to call them in Holland and explain what happened?'

'No, all three kids are here in Florence. They arrived yesterday.'

Or were they already here on Friday night? Warning bells started ringing in my head. Might the murderer be one of Berg's offspring, maybe keen to get hands on an inheritance? 'Where are they staying?'

'At the victim's home in Signa, not that far from your house. I've arranged to go around there to speak to them at ten o'clock this morning. I could probably find an interpreter by then, but if you felt like coming along, I'd be happier. I'd be grateful to have another pair of eyes on them.'

'Yes, of course, I'm only too pleased to help out, but what about Virgilio? Isn't he involved?'

There was a pause before Marco answered. 'I told the *commissario* about it, but he wasn't interested. He just told me to get on with it myself...' His voice tailed off uncertainly before he added, 'To be honest, Dan, I'm worried about him. He doesn't seem to be himself.'

This certainly wasn't news to me, but I remained non-committal for now. 'Maybe he's had a hard week. I hope he hasn't got a health problem.'

'I really don't know. I've been trying to get him to tell me what's bothering him, but he just clams up.' Another pause. 'You and he get along well. I don't suppose you feel like sitting down with him one of these days, do you? Maybe he might be prepared to tell you what's bugging him. I hope it's not me. I don't think I've made any serious blunders recently, but there's no mistaking the fact that he's uptight about something.'

I promised him that I would see what I could do and he sounded relieved. He dictated the victim's address to me and we agreed to meet there at ten. When I asked him whether he thought I should bring Oscar, he was all for it.

'Yes, bring him, by all means. We've got to give these people some pretty grim news, so they might appreciate having a friendly dog around.'

'Don't they know their father's dead?'

'Yes, but they don't know that he was murdered yet.'

I couldn't help adding, 'Unless one of them did it.'

'My thoughts entirely.'

Anna wasn't exactly happy, but at least she looked resigned when I told her I had to go off and help Marco. As for Oscar, he's always happy to go for a ride in the van – unless it's to the vet.

* * *

Signa is situated to the west of Florence, just past the last of the industrialised suburbs surrounding the city. The land there is predominantly flat, but there's a single hill dominating the little town and this overlooks the River Arno below. This hill is home to a number of wealthy Florentine families looking for some respite from the cloying heat that descends on the city when summer comes around.

David Berg's house was a delightful Tuscan villa set in its own gardens, and access from the road was up a private drive that curled up the hill to the house through olive trees and immaculately pruned shrubs. Close up, I could see that it wasn't a genuine old building, but an authentic-looking, twentieth-century reproduction of a traditional-style villa, complete with a dovecot in the middle of the roof, no doubt no longer housing doves, but serving as a spectacular lounge with panoramic views back towards Florence as far as the Duomo itself. Such a house in such a location was no doubt worth a lot of money and I wondered, not for the first time, who was going to inherit the old man's wealth.

Marco's squad car arrived thirty seconds after I did, just as I was opening the back door to let Oscar out of the van. The parking area was pretty full by now. Four cars were already parked outside the villa: an Italian-registered Fiat and three

Dutch-registered cars – a big BMW saloon, a Japanese SUV, and a Jaguar sports car. All these three vehicles looked nearly new, so clearly, the family had money.

Marco and I shook hands and headed up four stone steps to the front door. I couldn't help noticing no fewer than three CCTV cameras located at strategic positions around the exterior. This was a man who had liked his privacy.

The hefty wooden door was opened for us by a stern-looking woman dressed in black. In spite of the recent death of David Berg, I had the feeling that this was probably the way she normally dressed. Only her apron was white. She could have been anything from forty to sixty years old and she had one of those expressionless faces that could tell a lot of stories – but probably wouldn't say more than the bare minimum. She ushered us in, shooting Oscar a suspicious look as she did so, and informed us that, 'The family are in the lounge.' Maybe I was reading too much into her tone, but I got the impression that her opinion of 'the family' wasn't particularly high.

We found five people waiting for us in a large, high-ceilinged room with what looked like a genuine medieval stone fireplace – presumably sourced from an antiquarian – and a gleaming shield and two crossed swords mounted on the wall above the mantlepiece. The furniture was sturdy and traditional in design, mostly polished wood and leather. Oil paintings of Tuscan scenes lined the walls, and the floor was composed of pink marble tiles, strewn with fine-looking rugs. Whoever had furnished the place had obviously been a traditionalist.

The family was seated on two large, leather sofas: two men and a woman to our right and a couple to our left. They all looked as if they were in their thirties or forties. A bearded man on the right-hand sofa rose to his feet to greet us as Marco held up his warrant card. Like so many Dutch people, the man with the beard spoke fluent English with just a bit of an accent.

'Good morning. My name is Casper Berg. David Berg was my father.' He pointed to the woman beside him and the man seated alongside her. 'This is my wife, Helga, and my brother, Luuc.' He looked across towards the other sofa. 'That's my sister, Emma, and her partner, Guido.' Again, maybe it was just me, but I felt I could identify distaste in his voice when he mentioned the name of his sister's man.

As agreed with Marco, I stepped forward and introduced the two of us to them. 'This is Inspector Innocenti of the Florence police and my name is Dan Armstrong. I'm British, but I live here now and I'll be helping with the language.'

Casper Berg nodded and indicated a pair of armchairs. We sat down and I was pleased to see Oscar follow me over and take up station at my feet rather than try to jump onto anybody's lap. As Marco began to talk, I translated automatically and studied the family members more closely while I did so. Casper Berg, with his bushy, black beard, was probably in his late forties and was presumably the eldest of the siblings. He was tall and solidly built. His brother, Luuc, looked several years younger, and he had broad shoulders and strong forearms, while his sister, Emma, was quite a bit younger, maybe around thirty-five or -six. Her partner, Guido, was of a similar age. He had immaculately styled, dark hair, his clothes fitted him perfectly, and he had the superior expression of a man who knows he looks good. Emma was also good-looking, but not as attractive as Casper's wife, Helga, who appeared to be the youngest of the bunch, in spite of being married to the oldest sibling.

Marco broke the news to them that their father's death was being treated as murder, and I kept a close eye on the faces around me, looking for any signs of guilt. I saw none, but, interestingly, nobody in the room appeared to be particularly saddened by the death of the old man. Marco must have picked up on this, as his next question was one that I would have asked myself.

'Please can I ask how relations were between you all and Mr Berg?'

First, it looked as though Casper was going to answer, but his sister, Emma, spoke up before him. 'I think "non-existent" sums that up.' She spoke almost perfect English with a hint of an American accent. Marco asked her to elaborate and she did. 'He left us and divorced our mother when I was seven years old. That was almost thirty years ago and I hadn't seen him or heard from him since then until I received the invitation a month ago to come here.'

'And how did you feel when your father left home?'

She looked him square in the eye. 'How do you think it made me feel? He abandoned us. I was puzzled, unhappy and bitter.'

'And was that the same for all of you? You've had no contact with your father for thirty years?' All three siblings nodded and Marco continued. 'You all received invitations to come here?' The heads around us nodded again. 'And were you all equally estranged from him?' Again, the nods. 'Was this because of the divorce?'

Casper answered this time. 'Thirty years ago, our father took up with an Italian woman and abandoned us without a backward glance. I'm sure you can imagine the effect that had on our mother and on the whole family. He left Amsterdam for Italy, severed all links and I, for one, had no desire to see him again after the way he'd treated our mother – and us.'

'What about your mother? Does she still live in the Netherlands?'

'Our mother passed away four months ago and, yes, she'd been living in Amsterdam, like the rest of us.'

'So the invitations to come here suddenly appeared out of the blue after thirty years?' I echoed Marco's amazement in my voice as I translated his words. 'Did he give you a reason? After all, you answered the call, so presumably this was in response to something in his invitation.'

Emma nodded. 'The reason we all answered his summons is money, plain and simple. He told us he wanted to discuss our inheritance.'

Her brother, Luuc, spoke for the first time, reaching into his pocket and pulling out a letter, which he unfolded. He was a fit-looking man with close-cropped, dark hair, but his face was weary. Mind you, if he'd driven here from Holland, he had every right to look tired. He also looked displeased – whether at the death of his father or the intrusion of the police was hard to decipher.

'Our father indicated that he'd become a very wealthy man and he instructed us to come and hear how he intended to divide his estate.' He added extra emphasis to the word *instructed* and I deduced that this might be the explanation for his apparent displeasure. Presumably, he hadn't wanted to come at all.

He continued, 'All three invitations are identical and written in Dutch, but I can give you a translation into English if you like.' He also spoke excellent English. In response to Marco's nod of the head, he gave us the translation and I relayed it to Marco in Italian. The invitation was short, formal, and brief to the point of rudeness. A couple of lines struck me as I listened to the translation. These were, *I am aware of my advancing years and I need to get my affairs in order,* and, *I have amassed a considerable fortune and I wish to inform you of how I intend to distribute it.*

The invitation was simply signed, *David Berg, your father*. No terms of endearment. Icy cold.

Marco and I exchanged looks before he continued with his questions. 'How were relations between you and your mother?'

Luuc answered. 'We loved our mother dearly. She was treated terribly by our father, and we all stuck by her to the very end. Of course, there was no word from our father when she died.' His expression visibly softened when he mentioned his mother, but when he spoke of his father, it darkened. His brother and sister nodded in unison and Marco asked for more information.

'Your father had a jewellery business here in Florence. What did he do when he lived in the Netherlands?'

Casper answered. 'The same. He had three shops in the centre of Amsterdam. Luuc, Emma and I still work there now.'

'So your mother was well provided for.' Casper nodded reluctantly, and Marco tried another question. 'What about the woman he divorced your mother for? Is she still around? Have you met her?'

Luuc answered first, almost spitting. 'We haven't seen her and we have no desire ever to see her.'

They all shook their heads and Emma made a suggestion. 'Like Luuc says, we've never met her. If you want to know more about her, you probably need to ask Ines. She's worked here for almost twenty years.'

'Ines is the woman who showed us in?'

'Yes, she's the housekeeper.'

'When did you all arrive here?'

Casper took over again. 'We were given strict instructions to arrive yesterday at three o'clock – which we did. Ines let us in, but only an hour or two later, we received the news of the death of our father the previous night. Are you quite sure it was murder?

He was eighty-six, after all.' He sounded more frustrated than saddened.

Even so, Marco offered his condolences. 'I'm afraid there's no doubt about it. He was definitely murdered. I'm very sorry he died before you could see him again.'

Luuc gave a dismissive shrug of the shoulders. 'Speaking personally, I'm glad I didn't see him. I would have had nothing to say to him – at least nothing polite – and, to be honest, I didn't want to come here at all. I only came because Casper and Emma thought we should.'

Casper explained. 'After receiving the invitations, the three of us got together to decide what to do and we finally agreed that it was probably to our advantage to come.'

'Have you seen his will?'

They all shook their heads and Marco and I exchanged glances again. What was going through my head once more was the very important question of who stood to benefit from the old man's death. Could it be that his original will had left everything to his Italian partner, and when she had heard that he was planning on distributing his wealth among his children, she had taken drastic action to do away with him before he could make any changes and cut her out? Alternatively, was his killer sitting in front of me right now?

After a few more questions, Marco stood up. 'Obviously, the important thing now is to get hold of your father's will. I'll get my people to do this, unless you have any objections.' This was met with blank faces all round, so he closed his notebook. 'I'd like you all to stay here for the next couple of days. I'll need to speak to you again, but I won't keep you here any longer than I have to. As soon as I have details of the will, I'll be back in touch. Now I'd like to go and speak to the housekeeper.'

5

SUNDAY MID-MORNING

We left the family sitting there in silence and walked back to the entrance hall. There was a little hand bell on a side table and Marco picked it up and rang it. A few seconds later, the housekeeper appeared and headed for the front door.

'Are you leaving, gentlemen?'

Marco shook his head. 'Not yet, *signora*. First, I'd like to ask you some questions. Is there somewhere we can go?'

She turned back and led us along a short passage to the kitchen. Although the room had been designed to look like a traditional Tuscan farmhouse kitchen with hefty oak beams spanning the ceiling, there was a battery of modern kitchen equipment along one wall. We sat down around a fine old wooden table in the middle of the room and the housekeeper offered us coffee. While she made this with the aid of a professional-looking coffee machine, Marco embarked on the questions.

'I gather you're the housekeeper and you've worked here for twenty years. Is that correct?'

'That's correct. My name is Bianchi, Ines.'

'Thank you, Signora Bianchi. Is there a Signor Bianchi?'

She nodded. 'My husband works for a textile company in Prato. We live in Campi Bisenzio.' I recognised the name of a fairly unprepossessing suburb of Florence only a few kilometres from Signa.

'What hours do you work?'

'I used to come in at eight and leave at four but nowadays, I normally come in at midday. Signor Berg always leaves... left home at seven-thirty so there was no need to make breakfast for him. As a result, I spend the afternoons here and leave again at eight, after preparing his dinner. This weekend, because we have guests – and, believe me, that is very, very unusual – I'm here all day.'

'So having guests in the house was unusual? How unusual?'

'Extremely. There are six bedrooms here and, apart from Signor Berg's room, none of them have been used for years. The last time there was a guest here was probably four, five years ago – and only for a single night.'

'Can you remember who that was?'

'I don't think I ever heard his name, but he was a tall Dutchman – maybe about your age. He didn't speak Italian and he never said a word to me. He arrived one afternoon and left again early next day. He and Signor Berg spent hours locked in the study together, so it was clearly a business meeting.'

'We understand that Signor Berg originally moved from Holland thirty years ago with an Italian woman. Do you know her? Were they still a couple?'

'Yes, she lived here with him so I knew her well, but I'm afraid she died back before Christmas.'

I couldn't help reflecting on the synchronicity of both Berg's original wife and his Italian partner dying at almost the same time. 'Can you give me her name, please?'

'Greco, Claudia Greco.'

'Did they marry? Did they have a family?'

'No, they had no children and they lived together as man and wife, but without making it legitimate.' Ines Bianchi's tone expressed disapproval. 'Still, she was a good woman and she must have had the patience of Job to have stuck with him for so long.' She brought over two little cups of strong, black coffee and set them down on the table in front of us. 'He wasn't an easy man to get on with.' She hesitated before taking a seat at the end of the table. 'I know we shouldn't speak ill of the dead, but Signor Berg wasn't a very nice man.'

'In what way?'

'He was very selfish. All that counted for him was himself and his business.'

'Was it a big business? After all, it was only a small boutique on the Ponte Vecchio.'

She scoffed. 'It was a big business, all right. The shop was only the icing on the cake. His main activity was as a wholesaler of precious stones and precious metals. I can remember numerous occasions when he came home with a heavy bag and told me there were hundreds of thousands of euros' worth of gold or precious stones inside it.'

'Was it a common occurrence for him to bring high-value merchandise back here?'

'Maybe not every night, but he preferred to keep his valuables in the safe here, rather than at the Ponte Vecchio. As you came in, you maybe noticed the security system we have here. This place is like Fort Knox.'

'Do you think there's much in the safe now?'

'I have no idea. You should go and take a look for yourselves, but I'm not sure how you're going to get into it. I don't know the combination and, to the best of my knowledge, now that Signor

Berg's dead, neither does anybody else. I can let you into his study, but from then on, you're on your own.' She even managed a hint of a smile. 'I imagine you'll need dynamite.'

I saw Marco shoot a glance towards the kitchen door and he lowered his voice even though we were speaking Italian. 'Tell me about the family group who have assembled here. Presumably, Signor Berg must have informed you that they were coming.'

The smile disappeared from her face. 'Yes, he told me, last month in fact. From the way he spoke about them, I could tell he wasn't looking forward to seeing them but, considering that he went off and left his wife and children all those years ago and hasn't been back in touch with them since, I would imagine they felt very similarly about him. The one with the short hair, Luuc, in particular has been looking like a bear with a sore head.'

'Can you remember anything Signor Berg said about them? We're trying to work out exactly why he decided to restore contact with his children after so long. Was he maybe becoming a bit more mellow in his old age?' Although Marco already knew the answer to this one, he was clearly trying to see if Berg might have had an alternative reason for calling his children to join him, not just because of his last will and testament.

Ines shook her head decisively. 'Very much the opposite. The older he got, the more difficult he became.' She paused for thought while we sipped our scalding-hot, but very good, coffees. 'Knowing him, I imagine it was probably about money. It normally was with him. Maybe he wanted to talk to them about his will.'

Marco nodded. 'It could well be. By the way, can you give me the name of his lawyer and maybe his accountant?'

'His lawyer, yes: Emiliano Vicentino. His studio is in Florence, in Via Ricasoli. He came here two or three times a year, and the two of them would lock themselves in the office and talk for hours. As for an accountant, Signor Berg didn't have one. He did all that kind of thing himself. I imagine that was because he wouldn't trust anybody else to handle his money.'

'What about the family? How are you getting on with them?'

She shrugged. 'Considering that I don't speak Dutch, they don't speak Italian, and my English is seriously limited, you can probably imagine. They seem pleasant enough and, understandably, they've been looking very puzzled. They'd only just arrived yesterday afternoon when the news of their father's death came through and they were shocked. I was too, to be honest. He might have been old but he was tough. It wouldn't have surprised me if he'd lived to be a hundred.'

'Does it come as a surprise to you to know that he didn't take his own life? We now have evidence that he was murdered.'

The housekeeper nodded a couple of times but didn't look as surprised as we might have expected. 'I couldn't believe that he'd taken his own life. He seemed far too tough for that. I suppose it was a robbery, was it? I often wondered, considering that he used to carry such valuable items around with him, whether somebody would try to get their hands on them.'

'We're not sure at the moment. It happened inside his shop and there was considerable upheaval in there, so it's difficult to know what might have been taken. It happened on Friday evening. Were you aware that Signor Berg hadn't come home that night?'

'No. He'd told me the day before that he was going out somewhere that evening and I didn't have to prepare dinner for him. I came in a bit earlier than usual yesterday – around ten – as I had to prepare for the arrival of the family and there was no sign of him, so I just assumed he'd come home the night before and then gone off to work at seven-thirty as usual.'

'What did the family members do after hearing the news?'

'They haven't really done very much since then, apart from sit in the lounge and talk. I thought they might go out and visit Florence yesterday evening, but only Luuc has been out. The others have just been hanging around here. Presumably, their father's death has had its effect on them, even if he must have been a virtual stranger to them after so many years.'

Marco nodded a couple of times. 'I couldn't see any great signs of grief. What do you think, Signora Bianchi? Would you say that any one of them was particularly pleased or displeased at the news of the death?'

She shrugged. 'The language barrier is what it is but, like you, I didn't see any great sorrow on their faces – particularly not on the face of Luuc.' She produced a cloth from her apron pocket and absently wiped a microscopic speck of dust from the table-top. 'But, like I say, after thirty years apart, who can blame them?'

We carried on asking questions, but it soon became clear that there wasn't much more that Signora Bianchi could tell us. The old man had been secretive, uncommunicative and, by the sound of it, he had had next to no friends – and I was beginning to realise why. From what we'd been hearing, he hadn't been an endearing character. Finally, we asked to be shown up to his study on the first floor where Signora Bianchi produced a serious-looking key from the pocket of her apron, unlocked the door, and left us to it. I had to lean on the door to open it and, from its considerable weight, it was clear that it was armoured, faced with timber. We walked in and I pressed it closed behind us, hearing a solid clunk from the lock as I did so. I couldn't help noticing two hefty bolts on the inside so Berg could barricade himself inside if necessary. No doubt this room had been designed, not only as a study, but as a safe room.

The study was quite large, and there was another door at the far end – this time, a normal wooden one. Behind this, I found a serious steel safe the size of a fridge freezer. I tried turning the wheel on the front to open it but, as we'd been warned, this resisted all attempts. Above it, in the upper portion of the door, was a dial within a dial. I spun it a few times, hearing it click as it turned, but, without the combination, we had no chance of opening it. I went back into the study and headed for the huge mahogany desk with a swivel chair behind it. On the wall behind it was an oil painting that even I could see had been heavily influenced by Dutch landscape painters like Bruegel. It was a winter scene with people skating on an ice-covered canal and no doubt had reminded Berg of his youth in the Netherlands. It was a fine painting and I wondered idly if it might be valuable. Marco was sitting at the desk, searching through the drawers, so I flicked through the papers on the desktop. These were of little interest apart from a slim, beige file.

I took this to the window – which was criss-crossed with steel bars – and checked the contents in the sunlight. It quickly emerged that these were copies of the letters David Berg had sent to his children, inviting them to come to Florence, along with their replies. These were all in Dutch but I found them easy enough to decipher with the help of memories of German lessons at school many years earlier and an Italian-Dutch dictionary on a nearby shelf. The only item of particular interest was a simple piece of paper that looked as if it had been torn out of an exercise book. On it, there were letters in a list down the page, each one of them with a tick alongside it. These were C, L, E and EV.

It didn't take much deduction to work out that these stood for the names of the three siblings: Casper, Luuc and Emma, but it took me a moment or two to recognise the identity of the fourth. Presumably, EV had to be Emiliano Vicentino, the lawyer. Assuming that he, too, had been invited to the house for the meeting on Saturday afternoon, it appeared that the old man had intended to write – or more probably rewrite – his will there and then. This of course begged the question of whether the lawyer had answered the call to come here on Saturday afternoon as well. Nobody had mentioned him. I glanced across at Marco as he slid the last of the desk drawers shut and I held out the sheet of paper and the file towards him.

'Seems like the old boy preferred old-fashioned mail rather than the electronic variety.' I looked around the room. 'Which reminds me: no computer. I imagine he must have had one, but it isn't here. Maybe at the shop or even in the safe. Talking of the safe, how do you plan on opening it? Hopefully not dynamite.'

He smiled as he took the sheet with the initials on it from my hand. 'I'll let the tech people worry about that. If the worst comes to the worst, they'll have to contact the makers.' He pulled out his phone and glanced across at the formidable safe. 'I've a feeling it may take some time to get into that beast. I'd better get onto them right away. We also need to check with Berg's bank. You never know, there might be a piece of paper with the combination on it sitting in a safe deposit box.' He shot me a quick grin. 'The *commissario* always tells me I'm a hopeless optimist.'

I waited until he'd finished the call before making a suggestion. 'It might be an idea to ask the housekeeper if the lawyer showed up here yesterday. The family downstairs didn't mention him. And if he didn't come, was that because Mr Berg had told him to come at a later date, or might it have been because the lawyer knew that his client had been murdered? Maybe he even committed the crime himself, although until we can get into the safe, it's hard to come up with a motive.'

Marco leant against the side of the desk and looked across at me. 'What did you think of the family? It's quite clear there was no love lost between the old man and his kids, and who could blame them? Can you imagine going off and abandoning your children – one of them a seven-year-old – and not bothering to contact them for decades? He must have been a very odd character.'

'You can say that again. By the sound of it, his life was all about precious stones and precious metals. I have a feeling his death might have been all about that as well.'

Marco nodded. 'Robbery does seem the most likely motive, but from what the housekeeper said, it sounds as though he kept the more valuable items here in his safe.' I saw his eyes flick across to the bars on the window. 'Although getting access to them would have been a real challenge for any thief. What about the family? Did you think any of them looked suspicious?'

I shook my head. 'Not really. They all looked mystified. I wasn't too struck by Emma Berg's partner, Guido, but maybe that's just me. With a name like that, I wonder if he has Italian roots although, if he spoke the language, I would have expected him to have been able to act as interpreter for them. Otherwise, the only one that stood out was Luuc. I didn't immediately get any suspicious vibes from his brother and sister, but Luuc clearly had a serious grudge against his father.'

'My feeling exactly, but serious enough to contemplate patricide? Luuc definitely had no love for his father and no discernible grief at his demise. I know what you mean about Guido. I didn't like the look of him either, but that doesn't make him a murderer. But whether the kids liked the father or not, from what we've heard, the idea of this family meeting was so that Berg could prepare or change his will – presumably in favour of his children – so I'm at a loss to see any possible motive they might have had for killing him before he did that.' He looked up at me. 'Right?'

I nodded. 'Right. I don't see it either. From what the house-keeper said, Berg had precious few friends, although it would be worth checking up on his former partner who died last year.

Maybe there was a child – unknown to the housekeeper – who might have got wind of the old man's plan to change his will, which, presumably, would have benefitted her or her relatives.'

He stood up. 'Definitely, I'll go and have another word with the housekeeper now to check if the lawyer turned up yesterday afternoon. As far as he's concerned, I need to sit down and have a long talk to him. It sounds as though he knew the old man better than anybody, so maybe he can shed some light on what happened.'

I glanced at my watch. It was almost eleven. 'Well, good luck with it. I'd better get home to Anna, but if you need any more help, you know where I am.'

'Thanks, Dan, and you won't forget what I said about the boss, will you? Something's bugging him, and I'd dearly like to know what it is.'

'He and Lina came around for dinner last night and Anna noticed it too. I tried to get him to tell me what was on his mind, but he wouldn't say a word. I'll definitely have another try and I'll let you know if I discover anything.'

I had been thinking a lot about Virgilio's obvious unhappiness, but without coming up with a satisfactory explanation. Was he experiencing personal or family problems or was it work-related? If so, maybe this case might offer a way of getting closer to him and, hopefully, helping him.

6

SUNDAY LATE MORNING

I left Marco and as I drove home, I thought back to the scene in the villa. Five people, six including the housekeeper, but none with any discernible motive to commit murder. Berg had had few friends and his former partner was also dead so, unless some member of her side of the family turned up, our original supposition that David Berg's death had been aggravated robbery looked the most likely scenario. If we were lucky, the contents of the safe would provide the police with some useful leads. Thought of the police made me think of Virgilio again. We were all agreed that something was preying on his mind, but the question was how to get him to talk about it. As I crossed the bridge over the Arno and turned towards Montevolpone, I let my mind roam. What could be troubling him?

Somehow, I felt convinced that it had something to do with police work – although it was strange that Marco hadn't been able to shine any light on it. Considering that they both worked closely together, this was bizarre. If not work, then what? From everything Virgilio had said to me over the years that I'd known him, I felt sure that this wasn't a sign that there was discord between him and his wife. They had always struck me as a very happy couple and, as far as I knew, their two children were both doing well in their chosen careers. Of course it could be a health matter, but surely he would have spoken to Lina about it if he'd discovered he had a medical problem. It was unlikely to be financial trouble because he'd recently received promotion to *commissario* and that would have come with a corresponding increase in pay. I'd never known him to gamble and I thought it highly unlikely that he would have done anything illegal, so what could it be?

I called Anna back at my place to see what she thought I should do. Her answer was very simple.

'Go and talk to him. It's only eleven now, so he won't be having lunch yet. Why not drop round to his house and take him out for an *aperitivo* or a walk with Oscar? Go on, do it.'

She was right. We did need to talk, so I did a U-turn and headed back towards Florence. Virgilio's house is in Scandicci, which is roughly halfway between my house and the city centre, so it only took me ten minutes driving to get there. I was pleased to see his car parked outside the house, which boded well for my chances of finding him in. I parked behind it and Oscar and I went up to the front door. I pressed the bell and a few seconds later, it was opened by Lina. When she saw me, an expression of relief appeared on her face.

'*Ciao*, Dan, am I pleased to see you! He's spent half the night at his computer and he's back in his study now with the door closed. I wish he would tell me what's going on, but he just shakes his head and says he's fine.' She caught my eye and I could see the hurt and the worry in hers. 'But it's patently clear he's anything but fine. Would you like to have a try? He might talk to you.'

I gave her a reassuring hug. 'That's why I've come. I tried last night, but he wouldn't tell me a thing, so I thought I'd come here now to try again.'

She pointed up the stairs. 'You know where his study is, don't you?'

I left her there and set off up the stairs with Oscar. When I got to the door of his office, I stopped and tapped on it. 'Virgilio, it's me, Dan. Can I come in?' Just to add impetus to the request, Oscar stretched out a paw and scratched the bottom of the door. There was silence for a few moments before I heard footsteps approaching and then the key turned in the lock. I was still digesting the fact that he had locked himself in when the door opened and I was confronted by my friend. He looked awful. By the look of his crumpled T-shirt, he had probably slept in it, and his eyes were bloodshot. He blinked a few times and bent down to stroke Oscar's head.

'*Ciao*, Oscar. *Ciao*, Dan.' He sounded as weary as he looked.

I decided to take the bull by the horns. 'We need to talk. Can I come in?'

He stepped back and I entered the room, stopping to close the door behind me. I went over to the window, deliberately distancing myself from whatever he'd been doing on the computer, and turned towards him.

'We're all worried about you, Virgilio. I think it's time you talked to somebody, don't you?' Before he could retort, I carried on. 'You know me well enough by now. You can tell me anything and I promise I won't judge, I won't be shocked and, unless you agree, I won't tell a soul, and that includes Lina and Anna. Nobody, all right? Whatever it is that's bugging you, you need to talk about it. Please.'

I saw him slump down in his chair, but he gave no immediate reply. Oscar, working out that his good friend was struggling, wandered over and leant against his leg in a show of canine support. I had to wait almost a minute before Virgilio finally raised his eyes and spoke.

'Thanks, Dan. It was good of you to come. You're right, I do need to speak to somebody and, the more I think about it, you're just about the only person who can understand the complexity of the problem and who might be able to help. Most important of all, you're above suspicion.' His voice lapsed as he started to collect his thoughts but I remained silent, letting him take his time, wondering what his 'above suspicion' comment might presage. Finally, keeping his voice low, although we were alone in the room with the door closed, he started.

'There's something bad going on at work, something very bad.' I tried to keep my face as expressionless as possible while he went on. 'I've been suspicious for several months now, but it's becoming more and more evident that there's somebody on the force who's working for the other side.'

'When you say, "working for the other side", who is the other side and what's happening?'

'That's what I'm trying to find out. The most obvious thing I've found so far is that files are disappearing.'

This didn't sound good at all. 'But isn't everything on computer these days?'

'That's the problem. Not only are hard copies of files going missing, but records are being wiped from the system.'

This was sounding ominous now. 'What sort of records?'

He even managed an attempt at a wry smile. 'That's also the problem. The moment they disappear, they become almost impossible to trace. The first one I came across quite by accident two months ago. An asylum seeker was found stabbed to death at the main station, but it was never followed up. I only happened across it when I was checking a completely different case – the death of another asylum seeker – and saw it referenced. I've

spoken to the officer dealing with the first case and he confirms
he logged it and handed in his report, but somehow, that's gone
missing. Then last month, almost exactly the same thing
happened again – another stabbing and another file gone
missing.'

'But surely any officer who feels like it can't just wipe a file
without authorisation.'

He looked up at me, a haunted expression on his face. 'That's
what's worrying me, Dan; that sort of thing needs authorisation...
or it's being done by somebody high up. The more I look into it,
the more convinced I've become that it's being done by a senior
officer.'

I began to see why he was looking so worried. 'How senior?'

'Inspector or above.'

'What about somebody in IT?'

'They need to use a special code every time they log in, and
that keeps an exact record of what they've done and every file
they've accessed. I'm no computer genius but, as far as I can see,
the only person who could have done it has to be one of our
senior officers.'

I sat there and thought hard. Virgilio now occupied an important position in the Florence force and there were probably no
more than a handful of more senior officers between him and the
questore, the overall head of the force. There were probably
slightly more officers at inspector level but the total would only
amount to a dozen at most. This was serious. I looked across to
see him staring glumly at his computer screen.

'Do you have anybody particular in mind?'

He swivelled the laptop around so I could see the screen.
There were photos of the five most senior officers there and he
talked me through them.

'Parmigiano, Verdi, Grande, Romano and the *questore* himself,

Massimo Livornese. All senior officers. The *questore* has been in post for ten years now, Parmigiano and Romano have each been here for over thirty years. The other two have transferred in from other forces over the last few years. I know all five and up till now, I've had absolute trust in them. Now I find myself doubting all of them and it's driving me crazy. What do I do? I suppose I should go straight to the top and lay my suspicions before the *questore*, but what if he's the one? I could lose my job – or even my life – if he takes action to silence me.' He looked at me over the top of the screen. 'You see my problem?'

I certainly did. 'What about officers at inspector rank?'

'Five, three of whom are in areas like traffic or victim support. There are only two inspectors regularly involved with murder cases.'

And one of them was Marco. Suddenly, it became clear why Virgilio had been refusing to talk to his second-in-command about his suspicions. I decided to say it before Virgilio had to.

'There's Marco, but I would stake my life savings on him being straight. What about the other inspector? Do I know him or her?'

'Roberto Faldo, he's in murder as well but he tends to specialise in robbery. He joined us last year from Parma.'

'Who's your money on? The new boy, Faldo, or somebody more senior?'

He shrugged helplessly. 'I've been trying to narrow it down and I've come up with three probables – although any of the others could still be in the running. I know the *questore* and I feel as sure as I can be that I trust him. Yes, he can be an awkward character, but I can't see him betraying the force, *his* force. I know Parmigiano and Romano even better – we've pretty much grown up together and I would trust either of them with my life – so that leaves us with Verdi and Grande. At inspector level, there are the two: Faldo and, of course, Marco, although, like you, I can't imagine Marco being involved in anything illegal.'

I gave it a few seconds and then asked the inevitable question. 'So what's your next step?'

He rolled his eyes. 'That's what I've been trying to decide. The more I think about it, I reckon I have to go straight to the *questore*, don't you?' He caught my eye. 'What do you think I should do, Dan? Did you ever come up against anything like this?'

The answer to this was yes, sort of. I had come across a handful of bent coppers in my time and I knew that no force was without them. I tried desperately to think what support I could offer my friend. 'Yes, I've encountered rotten apples a few times but never at a very senior level. I remember a sergeant and four constables when I was in South-East London. They were running a very lucrative protection racket, milking shopkeepers for money every month. We'd heard rumours for ages, but every time we thought we were getting close to catching the perpetrators, the trail would go cold. In the end, the only conclusion we could draw was that it had to be an inside job. The boss assembled a small group of officers and swore us to secrecy. Between us, we kept a close eye on the affected premises until a uniformed constable popped up one day to collect. We followed him back to the station and managed to film him handing over the cash to the sergeant. After that, we were able to roll up the whole gang. Two of them got jail terms and all five were kicked off the force.'

As I was speaking, an idea occurred to me. 'In the first instance, if you like, I could take a look at the main suspects. Give me their details and I'll sit down at the computer and go through them one by one, looking into their personal lives, finances, backgrounds and so on. Normally, there's a reason why an officer goes bad – gambling or other debts, marital troubles and the like – and I might just uncover something.'

Virgilio gave me a grateful look. 'That's what I've been trying to do, but I know you're a whole lot better at this computer stuff than I am. Normally, I would just hand it over to our tech people, but I've no way of knowing if any of them are involved. That would be brilliant, Dan, if you can spare the time.'

I smiled at him in return. 'That's what friends are for.'

Although I was smiling, I was turning over in my head the possible ramifications if we were to discover something decidedly dodgy going on. Who could tell how far up the ladder the contagion might have spread?

7

SUNDAY AFTERNOON

I spent that afternoon at the computer, working my way through the list of Virgilio's possibles, but without uncovering anything particularly compromising. I started at the bottom with Inspector Roberto Faldo. He was forty-one years old and had been born in Parma, roughly a couple of hours up the autostrada to the north of Florence. He had attended Parma University before joining the police there. He was married with two teenage children and had been a police officer for almost eighteen years, moving to the Florence force eighteen months previously. Photos of him showed him to be a smart, fit-looking man and he appeared to be a motivated and ambitious officer who promised to go far.

The two more senior officers were both in their sixties. Vincenzo Grande, now sixty-one, had joined the police at the age of twenty-five and had spent most of his career in his native Sicily before getting his current position here in Florence as *Commissario Capo*, the next step up from Virgilio, and roughly equivalent to superintendent in the UK police. He was married with two sons and three grandchildren. When I saw his photo, I remembered meeting him on a couple of occasions. He had been cordial and welcoming and he certainly hadn't struck me as being devious, although I had struggled to understand his strong Sicilian accent.

His superior, the *vice questore*, occupied the position of second-in-command of the force and had come from Rome four years earlier. His surname was Verdi and I had never met him, but his parents might well have had an interest in music as they'd christened him Giuseppe, like the composer. He was sixty-three years old and married, but without children and, to the best of my knowledge, he had never written any operas. Both of these men were clearly career officers who had worked their way up through the ranks.

Once I'd established their identities, I set about doing a bit of digging into the past of all three men. Inspector Roberto Faldo was the easiest. Although he didn't have a social media presence, both of his teenagers did, and I was able to track the family back over the past five or six years of sports competitions, school plays and holidays as far away as the USA and Africa as well as closer to home on the Tuscan coast and the island of Elba. His hobby appeared to be sport in general in all its iterations. There were photos of Roberto on skis high in the mountains, in a battered 4 x 4 climbing a near vertical slope, standing on a podium in cycling gear, and crossing the finishing line of a triathlon. There were shots of him with his wife at various parties and other events, and she always had a broad smile on her face. Nothing sinister there. It looked like a solid, happy family.

Superintendent Vincenzo Grande, Virgilio's immediate superior, was less visible on the Internet but I managed to dig up some scraps of information. It was immediately clear that his hobby was hunting and I found references to him in connection with a hunting club by a lake to the west of Florence as well as another club dedicated to hunting for wild boar – a major pest in the Tuscan countryside. There were various photos of him with trophies and more bloodthirsty shots of him posing alongside the bodies of a variety of unfortunate dead animals. I knew from experience how popular hunting was here in Tuscany – in season, it often sounded like World War Three outside my house on a Sunday morning. No doubt Grande had quickly made friends with like-minded people after arriving here from Sicily. But as far as my investigation was concerned, unless you happened to be a wild animal, there was little about him of a negative nature to be found online.

Vice Questore Verdi was tall, meticulously groomed and always impeccably turned out. Online, he appeared at numerous formal events, even shaking hands with the president of the republic on one occasion, inspecting new recruits at a police college and appearing on several TV talk shows answering questions about law and order. His wife appeared only once – a grey-haired woman looking uncomfortable in an unflattering evening dress – but there appeared to be no shortage of younger, prettier women only too happy to be photographed alongside Giuseppe Verdi – composer or not.

From there, I moved on to less conventional searches, trying to discover if any of the three had skeletons in their cupboards of an illegal, financial or extramarital nature. Again, I drew a blank. I ran their names across the national and local news agencies without anything sinister being thrown up. There was an interesting article from a major Sicilian newspaper a few years back detailing Vincenzo Grande's successful steering of an *Antimafia* campaign – only a matter of months before he had obtained his present position here in Florence. The synchronicity of the timing struck me as interesting – had he applied for the Florence position so as to put five hundred miles between himself and the

Sicilian Mafia heartland? Had he, maybe, annoyed one of the local dons and had chosen retreat as the better part of valour?

I could find no dirt on the *vice questore* apart from what looked like a particularly intimate shot of him standing beside a young female officer in uniform, his arm around her waist and his hand resting cosily against her hip. She looked happy enough, and I could find nothing anywhere about him objectifying or abusing women, but I filed that away as a possible chink in his armour. However, what possible connection there might be between a womanising older man and a dead asylum seeker was beyond me.

I finally gave up, unable to find anything that might indicate guilt for any of the three. Of course, if the investigation had been carried out by the police, they would have been able to gain access to the bank accounts of the three men, which might have made interesting reading. Without that information, I had pretty much got as far as I could go. A quick flick through the other officers Virgilio had mentioned also produced nothing, so mid-afternoon, I picked up the phone and called Virgilio to break the news to him that I'd drawn a blank. He listened to me rattle off what little I'd managed to learn about them and his tone was gloomy when he answered.

'Thanks a lot, Dan, that's pretty much the same result that I've had. You're definitely right about one thing: Verdi, the *vice questore*, does have a reputation for having wandering hands, particularly with attractive, young, female officers. There have been a few grumbles but nobody's come forward to lodge an official complaint and I don't blame them. High-ranking officers like him have powerful friends.'

The Metropolitan Police has had its fair share of sexual predators – and quite probably still does – and one of the things in my career that I'm most proud of is managing to get justice for a young constable who had been stalked and sexually assaulted by a superintendent in – of all things – the vice squad. The super had been thrown out of the force but, sadly, the constable had subsequently also left, disillusioned, looking for a different career. I took an immediate dislike to the *vice questore*. Abuse of power is bad, but when it becomes sexual abuse, that's even worse. Whover the perpetrator was, I was determined to help Virgilio, so I came up with a suggestion.

'There's no way I can get access to your system so as to investigate serving police officers from within. That'll have to be up to you. If you want my advice, if I were you, I'd take Marco into my confidence. He's a good man and you can trust him, I'm sure. Anyway, that's your call, but what I could do if you like is to take a look at Verdi, Grande and Faldo *outside* work. Let me have their addresses and I'll do a little bit of discreet surveillance. You never know, we might catch one of them dipping his hands in the till.'

Virgilio gave me the addresses and thanked me but warned me to be as careful as possible. I promised that I would be the soul of discretion. He and I knew that it was unlikely that I'd be able to uncover anything to link any of the three men with missing police records, but it was worth a try.

I went out to where Anna was sitting under the pergola with Oscar sprawled at her feet. She was reading a hefty old tome even bigger than last night's steak. I glanced at the title and was unsurprised to see that it dealt with the life of her beloved Medici family, who had ruled Tuscany from the fifteen hundreds to the middle of the eighteenth century. She glanced up as she heard me, and Oscar also looked up, no doubt hoping for a walk or a biscuit – or both.

'Finished your investigation, Sherlock?' She gave me a smile. 'Normal people take time off to relax on a Sunday afternoon.'

Although over lunch, I'd told her that Virgilio was okay and that we'd had a good talk, I hadn't given her so much as a hint as to the true nature of his concerns, and she hadn't asked. I smiled back and indicated the book on the table in front of her.

'Look who's talking. You never stop working.'

She reached up and caught my hand. 'We're obviously made for each other.'

I leant down and gave her a kiss before pointing up the hill. 'Feel like coming for a walk?'

She had only just started to shake her head when there was a movement at her feet and Oscar leapt up 'Walk' is another trigger word for him, but he had to wait while I changed into shorts and trainers before we set off. In the winter, Florence is as cold as London or colder, and in the summer, temperatures regularly soar into the mid- or high thirties. Today was perfect. It was warm, probably in the low twenties, but the air was still fresh and the ground had dried out after Friday night's rain. It was an ideal afternoon for walking and chasing sticks – that's Oscar who does the chasing. I just throw them for him.

We walked up past rows of vines that were just beginning to show distinct signs of awakening from their winter sleep, and through olive groves where the nets used by the farmers when harvesting the olives in late autumn were still lying about. I buy oil and wine locally and both are excellent. The oil here in particular is so very different from most extra virgin olive oil on sale in UK supermarkets. This stuff is a deep-green colour and cloudy, not dissimilar in appearance to what comes out of an engine after twenty or thirty thousand miles. The taste is strong and fruity and it catches your throat when it's been freshly pressed. One of my favourite snacks is simply a thick-cut slice of the wonderful unsalted Tuscan bread, rubbed with a clove of garlic, then liberally drizzled with freshly pressed oil and sprinkled with a pinch of salt. With a glass of Chianti, it's unbeatable.

My gastronomic musings were interrupted by my phone. It was Marco and he had news.

'*Ciao*, Dan, I haven't been able to contact Berg's lawyer yet, but listen to this: the housekeeper says the lawyer came for dinner on Wednesday, three days *before* the family get-together. Are you thinking what I'm thinking?'

I certainly was. 'Assuming that the lawyer didn't just come to give advice, this could mean that Berg actually changed his will in advance of seeing his children. Did he change it to benefit his kids as they anticipated? Alternatively, now that his long-term girlfriend has died, did he disinherit the family and arrange to give the whole lot to the Italian equivalent of Battersea dogs' home?'

I heard him chuckle. 'I'm sure the Ente Nazionale Protezione Animali would be only too happy to receive a hefty legacy, but could he really disinherit his kids? It depends whether his affairs are going to be treated under Italian law or Dutch law. I would imagine, seeing as he's been resident here, that it will be Italian law and, as such, there's a fixed percentage that has to go to each of his kids, irrespective of whether he liked them or not. Besides, whatever the legalities of his will and the fact that he hasn't contacted his children for thirty years, cutting them out of their inheritance would strike me as downright malicious.'

'Everything I've heard about him so far tells me that he was a strange and selfish man, so that might have been his plan. Maybe he blamed them for not making the effort to try to contact him, and this would have been his idea of revenge. Of course, until we get sight of the will, there's no way of knowing.'

'Exactly, and most probably the will's locked inside the safe at his villa – and things aren't looking too good on that front. The tech guys have just called me back to report that it's a Zugtresor safe, made in Switzerland, and virtually uncrackable. They've messaged the company to ask how to proceed, but it'll take time. Forensics are still combing the shop on the Ponte Vecchio and they report no sign of Berg's laptop or his phone. They've managed to open the safe there – like I told you, they described it as ancient and unsophisticated – but it only contained a few trays of fairly cheap rings and a collection of run-of-the-mill bracelets and necklaces. No sign of the entry combination to the safe at the villa. I'll contact his bank and his lawyer first thing tomorrow in the hope that they hold a copy of the will, or even the safe combination, but I doubt it. Clearly, the old man didn't trust a soul. We've released the victim's name to the media with a plea for anybody with any information to come forward but, again, I'm not holding my breath.'

'Have the media been informed that it's being treated as murder, not suicide?'

'Yes, and I've already had local TV trying to interview me. I wish the *commissario* could deal with them. I'm useless in front of a camera. Have you had a chance to talk to him yet?'

I decided to dodge the question. 'I'm waiting for the right opportunity. What about the late Claudia Greco, Berg's lady friend? Any luck tracing her family?'

'We're still looking into it, but it turns out she was originally from Naples and it appears that she had no family living near here and possibly none down there either. We're still checking, but it's not looking likely that there's a relative with a grudge who might have taken the law into his own hands.'

I could hear the frustration in his voice and it mirrored my own. 'So it's looking ever more likely that it was either a robbery that went wrong, or murder by person or persons unknown...' A thought occurred to me. 'What about CCTV? Surely the Ponte Vecchio must be bristling with cameras.'

'That's the other thing I wanted to tell you. A number of the jewellery shops on the bridge have CCTV as part of their security systems. Tech have been examining the footage and we now know one thing: the murderer was there, lying in wait, when Berg returned to his shop at 20.17 on Friday night, presumably straight after talking to you. The bad news is that it was dark by then and the perpetrator was wearing a hoodie. It looks like a man, taller than the victim, but that's about it. As Berg opens the door to the shop, the killer appears from the shadows, bustles him inside and closes the door behind them. Then there's no further sign of activity until 01.46 when the man in the hoodie emerges from the shop, carrying a coil of rope. There's still a surprising number of people about, so he lurks in the shadows for a bit until he spots his chance. He ties one end of the rope to a metal ring set in the wall, returns to the shop and reappears with one arm around the victim, supporting the body against his own as if the man's the worse for drink. He waits until a group of Fiorentina supporters go past and then he slips the noose around Berg's neck, pushes him off the edge, and disappears in the direction of the Pitti Palace.'

I did my best not to let my mind rest too much on the brutal way David Berg's life had ended. It wasn't the most sadistic murder I'd come across in my time but, considering that the victim had been an old man, it had to be the work of somebody with a very different moral compass from most people. He deserved to be caught and locked away for a very long time.

'When you say "disappears", weren't you able to track him on the city video surveillance system?' Florence has well over a thousand video cameras scattered about the city, making it theoretically feasible to track a person right across town – but not in this case.

Marco sounded puzzled and annoyed when he answered. 'Tech have tracked him going around the back of the Uffizi but not emerging again. In spite of the weather and the late hour, there were still quite a few people milling about, and all Tech can imagine is that he did a quick change and mingled with one of the groups. I don't know how he did it, but he just vanished.'

'That sounds very professional. The more I think about it, the more I reckon Berg's death was the work of a pro. Did you see anything that might help to identify the killer?'

'From the width of the shoulders and his way of walking, Tech are confident it was a man, not a woman, and they reckon he was between one metre eighty and one-eighty-five tall, but that's that. His clothes were dark and he was wearing gloves but nothing else of note – no wristwatch, no earring, no distinctive shoes, nothing.'

I felt as frustrated as he did. I'm six foot one, which is about one metre eighty-five, and I know how many men there are in the world of my height, plus or minus an inch or two. Looking for a needle in a haystack didn't even begin to describe it. 'He obviously came prepared and he carried out his plan to perfection.' I did a quick bit of mental arithmetic. 'The fact that he spent five or six hours in close proximity to a dead body makes me think that we have to be talking about a pro. Either it was a robber with a strong stomach or the victim was deliberately targeted by a professional hitman. The question, of course, is why? Robbery is self-explanatory, but murder? What could that old man have done for somebody to put out a contract on him?'

8

MONDAY MORNING

I went into the office at just before nine on Monday morning and found Lina already there. She mustered a smile for Oscar and me, but I could see that the strain was beginning to show. I hadn't been able to tell her much yesterday after talking to Virgilio and all I could do today was smile back and offer a few words of encouragement.

'I'm sure Virgilio will get things sorted out very soon. Don't worry, it's nothing personal, it's just a work thing, and I've said I'll give him a hand if he needs me.' She looked slightly heartened so I changed the subject. 'What's in the diary for this week?'

She pressed a key and studied her computer screen. 'You're getting a visit at ten this morning from a Mr Jacobs. No idea what it's about. He called first thing this morning to make the appointment. He doesn't speak any Italian and he spoke English with a strong accent, so I wonder if he might be American. Then, tomorrow, you're spending the morning at the theatre – I couldn't get much out of them, but it sounds as though something fishy is going on. You have to meet a person called Zebra – that's the only name she gave me – in a café near the theatre at ten-thirty. It all sounds a bit weird. And there was a message from the mayor's secretary ten minutes ago. Please will you call as soon as you can?' She smiled. 'I saw him at your party on Friday night. Maybe he's offering you a place on the city council.'

I went into my office and called the number Lina had given me. With everything that had happened this weekend, I'd almost forgotten about the meeting I was supposed to have with him and, as I waited on the line, listening to soothing music and a voice telling me how important my call was to them, I wondered yet again what might be behind this. Was it personal, work-related, or something else?

A minute later, I was through.

'Good morning, this is the office of the mayor. How can I help?' She sounded cordial but businesslike.

I gave her my name and told her I'd been instructed to call back. She immediately recognised my name. 'Good morning, Signor Armstrong, the mayor asks if you would be free for lunch today.'

'Yes, indeed. What time and where?'

She told me twelve-thirty and gave me the name of a restaurant that was unfamiliar to me. When I checked it afterwards, I was impressed to see that it appeared to be an ordinary trattoria in a side street not far from the university where Anna worked. During my career at the Met, I'd lunched a few times with political figures and, without exception, had found myself in the sort of expensive, central London restaurant where I had been very relieved not to be picking up the bill. Either Mayor Gallo was a refreshingly frugal politician or he was deliberately meeting me in a place where he was unlikely to meet any of his peers. The plot thickened.

I spent half an hour on the computer, among other things checking out the theatre where I would have to go the next day.

Although I was familiar with the big-name theatres here in Florence like the Teatro Verdi or Teatro Puccini, I was unfamiliar with the name Teatro dell'Arno. I discovered that it was on the outskirts of the city and, by the look of it, it was housed in a former factory building or warehouse. The outside was spartan and decidedly unprepossessing and I found a couple of interior shots that looked little better. There was none of the baroque excess of red velvet and gilded luxury to be found in Italy's more famous theatres and opera houses. This was art on a budget. I wondered idly how somewhere like this managed to survive in the midst of the current financial crisis.

I also plotted the addresses of the three senior police officers on a map of the city. Inspector Faldo lived in the suburbs to the west of the city, coincidentally not that far from where Virgilio himself lived, and the other two had addresses inside the *centro storico*. Giuseppe Verdi, the *vice questore*, actually lived barely a three-or-four-minute walk from my office, while Vincenzo Grande's home was to the west of the main station, not far from the river. I resolved to spend a couple of hours that afternoon taking a close look at the properties in question and maybe, if I was lucky, I might find some helpful neighbours who could dish the dirt – although at this stage, I had little idea what sort of dirt I was looking for.

At five to ten, Lina buzzed me to say that Mr Jacobs had arrived and I went out to Reception to greet him. I found a thin older man, probably in his early seventies. His skin was pale – as if he rarely went outdoors – and he was walking with the aid of a stick. He looked frail, but the expression on his face was determined and I was reminded of my first and only impression of David Berg. I gave the man a welcoming smile and held out my hand.

'Mr Jacobs? I'm Dan Armstrong, how can I help?' As Lina had told me he spoke English, I addressed him in my own language.

He shook my hand and shot a wary glance across at Lina before answering. Nodding towards the open door to my office, he lowered his voice. 'Maybe I should explain it to you in your office.' He spoke very fluent English with what sounded like a Dutch accent, not dissimilar to Casper Berg. My curiosity was immediately aroused. If he did turn out to be Dutch, this would be quite a coincidence, and in my line of business coincidences aren't always what they seem.

'Of course.' I ushered him inside and made a show of shutting the door firmly behind me before taking a seat at my desk with him on the chair opposite me. Oscar looked up from his basket, saw that my guest wasn't female and relapsed into slumber once more. 'Now, Mr Jacobs, why don't you tell me all about it?'

He leant towards me, still keeping his voice low. 'I would like you to look into a suspicious death.'

'I see. How long ago did this suspicious death take place?' This wasn't the first time I'd been contacted to investigate events that had happened in the past, in some cases way back in the past, but his answer came as a surprise – though maybe not such a major surprise as all that.

'Friday night.'

'Three days ago? Surely, that's a matter for the police.' This was definitely sounding familiar and I had a feeling I knew what his answer to my next question was going to be, but I knew I had to ask it anyway. 'Can you give me the name of the victim?'

'Berg, David Berg. He's... he was a jeweller on the Ponte Vecchio.'

For now, I didn't repeat my comment about this being a matter for the police. I was far too interested to see if this unexpected visitor might be able to shed fresh light on Friday night's events on the Ponte Vecchio. 'Can I ask what your connection with the victim was?'

'Business. We did business together.'

'So are you in the jewellery trade?' He nodded and I went on. 'Did you know him personally? Had you met before?'

It seemed to me that he hesitated just a fraction too long before shaking his head. 'No, we'd just been doing business over the Internet.'

'When did you find out that he'd been killed?'

Again, just a hint of hesitation. 'This morning. I saw it on local TV.'

'You speak Italian?'

'Only a few words, but I recognised his photo and understood enough to gather that he'd hung himself.'

'If it was suicide, what makes you think it was suspicious?'

'He wasn't the sort of man to take his own life.'

'I'm sorry, but how can you say that if you've never met him?'

A nervous tic appeared at the side of his mouth and we both realised that he'd been caught out. After a longish pause, he looked up and nodded a couple of times. 'All right, I knew him, quite well in fact. We worked together for three years a long time ago, but the reason I told you I didn't know him was because I didn't want to get involved.'

'I can understand that, Mr Jacobs. But, by coming to me, surely you *are* getting involved, aren't you? Why not just let the police deal with it?'

'It's complicated. Listen, it's like this: I had an appointment with him on Friday evening. We arranged to meet at a restaurant called il Fiume at eight-thirty, but he didn't show. I called him several times but there was no reply, so I waited almost an hour, had a steak, and went back to my hotel.'

I asked him for his full name – Axel Jacobs – his phone

number, and the name of his hotel, which I recognised as a pricey four-star hotel bang in the centre. The restaurant where he had been supposed to meet Berg was also in the higher price bracket. This wasn't budget tourism. Then I asked him the obvious question.

'Why come to me, not the police? I imagine they'd be very pleased to hear from you.'

A more cautious expression appeared on his face and, after a long pause, he owned up.

'The fact is that Berg had something of mine and that's not the police's business. I paid him for it on Thursday and he was hanging onto the goods for me until Friday evening but, like I said, when I went to the restaurant on Friday night, there was no sign of him or of my property.'

'Can I ask what this property consisted of?'

His face hardened. 'No, you can't. All I'm prepared to tell you is that it's very valuable and, seeing as Berg and I are both in the jewellery trade, I'll let you work it out for yourself.'

'Can you at least tell me what it looks like?'

'It's inside a wooden cigar box – Cuban Montecristo No. 4. That's all I'm prepared to tell you at this stage.'

I was tempted to press him for more detail but decided to leave it for now. A cigar box would easily be big enough to hold a small fortune in gold or precious stones. 'I see. Would I be right in thinking that your interest in Mr Berg's death is not so much with what happened to the man as with trying to recover your property?'

'I'm sorry he's dead, but you're right, I want what's mine.'

'And you don't want to go to the police?'

He shook his head decisively. 'No, that's why I came to you. I'm prepared to pay you handsomely for your time, but if you feel you don't want to get involved then I'll be on my way.' He made to stand up, but I waved him back into his seat again. The fact that he didn't want the police involved struck me as decidedly dodgy, and under normal circumstances, I wouldn't have touched a case like this with a bargepole, but for now, I had no intention of letting him get away. His evidence was potentially far too important.

'It's all right, Mr Jacobs, what you do is up to you. I just think that you might get your property back sooner if you got the police involved.' He shook his head again so I moved on. 'You mentioned that you used to work with Mr Berg. Where was that and what were you both doing?'

'He was a diamond cutter and I worked alongside him in Amsterdam a long time ago. I'm Dutch.'

'And is that what you do now?'

'No, I don't cut any more; I trade in gold and precious stones nowadays.'

'And David Berg has been one of your trading partners? Did you come here often to visit him?'

'Not often. In fact, I haven't been to Florence for quite a few years. He used to come to the Netherlands quite frequently, so there was no need.'

'Were you buying or was he?'

'In this case, I was.' He could see that I wanted more so, grudgingly, he elaborated. 'I live and work in Antwerp. I don't know if you're familiar with the city, but it's the main European hub for the trade in precious stones and gold. I buy and sell gold and jewels. Berg bought from me, I bought from him, and we then sold to traders and retailers all over Europe.'

'So you're both wholesalers?'

He nodded.

'And, in consequence, I imagine you deal in pretty large

sums.' I caught his eye. 'I can see why you're so keen to get your property back. Was it gold that you were buying?'

'Something like that.' He sounded non-committal.

'Then surely you should go to the police. If they haven't already done so, I'm sure they'll have access to the victim's accounts and whatever he kept in his safe. They should be able to identify your property and let you have it back.'

The Dutchman's expression became more guarded. 'The fact is that I'm quite sure Berg wouldn't have wanted the police to look into his accounts and the same applies to me. He and I had what you might call a gentleman's agreement and not everything was written down, if you understand me.'

I certainly did – but to what extent either Berg or Jacobs qualified as gentlemen was another matter. 'I can see that you might have a problem. Your property may turn out to be in Berg's safe, but without any paperwork to support your claim, you'll struggle to prove that you've paid for it and it's yours. Give me a rough idea of value. Are we talking thousands, tens of thousands, hundreds of thousands of euros?'

His eyes flicked nervously towards the door. Seeing it still firmly closed, he took heart and looked back at me. 'Roughly three hundred thousand euros.' His expression hardened again. 'But that information stays between the two of us, right?'

I mulled this over for a few moments. 'So what exactly would you like me to do, Mr Jacobs? You asked me if I could investigate a suspicious death. Are you afraid that Berg was murdered by a thief who took your property?'

'The shop's closed and there's police tape across the door. I assume that's where it happened, so robbery strikes me as a logical assumption.'

I didn't tell him that this was the conclusion to which Marco and I had already come. There was no need for Jacobs to know that I was already closely involved in the investigation. 'You said Berg was going to give you your property on Friday night. Do you think he was keeping it in his shop? I imagine there's a safe there.' I already knew that there was one, but Marco had told me that Forensics had found little of great value inside it. No wonder Berg had kept his more valuable items in the serious safe back home. 'That's what you're afraid of, isn't it?' He nodded so I went on. 'If your property has been stolen, that means you could be three hundred thousand euros worse off. Were you insured?'

He gave me what my gran would have described as an old-fashioned look. 'This particular consignment wasn't insured because it never existed, if you see what I mean. And as for being worse off, I stand to lose not only the contents of the cigar box but also the payment I have already made.'

I saw quite clearly. This had been an undercover transaction, no doubt unbeknown to the taxman. Of course, I was no longer in the police so I let the implications of this slide. 'Have you any idea who might be responsible, either for the robbery, or Berg's murder, or both? Presumably very few people knew about this business transaction.'

'*Nobody* knew about this transaction.' He thumped his fist on the desk unexpectedly hard, enough to make Oscar open his eyes and look up with a mildly miffed expression at the disturbance to his beauty sleep. 'It must have been an opportunist thief.'

'If that's the case, I'm afraid it's going to be hard for me or the police to discover the identity of the perpetrator. Are you sure there wasn't somebody, anybody, who knew about your transaction?' Seeing him shake his head, I asked another question. 'Can you tell me how come you were prepared to leave Mr Berg with your cigar box and your three hundred thousand euros? That seems very trusting of you.'

He smiled back at me – although the smile was closer to a

grimace. 'I don't trust many people but, like I told you, David Berg and I go way back. I brought him payment on Thursday, took a look at the goods, and then asked him to keep everything in his safe while I spent Friday wandering around Florence. We've done it before and there's never been any bother.'

'How did you make the payment? Was it a cheque or draft that had to clear, or did you bring cash?' For what sounded like a dodgy deal, it occurred to me that it had most probably been cash, but I turned out to be wrong.

'Not exactly.'

'Not cash? It sounds as though you aren't talking about money. What did you give him as payment for the contents of the cigar box?'

He sighed. 'I can't see that it's any business of yours but, if you must know, I paid him in gold bullion.'

'I see.' I didn't know what else to say. This meant that Jacobs had travelled to Florence carrying three hundred thousand euros in gold bullion – uninsured gold bullion. He was either a very brave or a very foolhardy man – and he looked far from foolhardy.

'How long are you planning on staying in Florence?'

'I was going to leave on Saturday, but now I'll stay for as long as it takes.' He gave me a long, appraising look. 'I'll make a deal with you, Mr Armstrong: if you can get me my gold or my goods back without the police being involved, I'll pay you 10 per cent as a finder's fee; that's thirty thousand euros. I can't say fairer than that, can I?'

I had to agree. 'That seems fair.' Although 10 percent of the profits of a dodgy deal didn't really sit well with me after a lifetime of enforcing the law. I told myself that I would have time to wrestle with my conscience if the money ever materialised – and my feeling was that Jacobs was going to struggle to get his hands on his property again.

What he said next was anything but fair.

He stood up and held out his hand. 'But let's be quite clear about something. What I've told you is in confidence. If you start blabbing to anyone, you'll regret it. Seriously.'

'That sounds like a threat, Mr Jacobs.' Although he didn't look strong enough to threaten anybody, maybe he had some unpleasant friends.

'Good, it was meant to be. Now, are you going to shake on the deal or not?'

9

MONDAY LUNCHTIME

I tried calling Marco to pass on this latest information but just got his answerphone. I left a message for him to contact me and then gave Oscar a quick walk followed by his all-important food before leaving him with Lina while I went for lunch with the mayor.

The restaurant he had chosen was called La Vecchia Stalla, which translates as the Old Cowshed or Stables and it was about five hundred metres from Anna's university, just outside the *centro storico*. It was a fifteen-minute walk from my office and on the way, I phoned and left a message for Virgilio, telling him I would take a look at the residences of his suspects later that afternoon. No sooner had the call ended than my phone started ringing again. It was Marco, returning my call and passing on news of his own.

'*Ciao*, Dan. Bad news, I'm afraid. David Berg didn't have a safe deposit box at the bank, so no help with finding the combination to get into the big safe at his villa. Tech have heard back from the safe makers in Switzerland and they're going to send one of their experts. Unfortunately, they can't get here until tomorrow or Wednesday, so we just have to be patient.' He lowered his voice. 'Thanks for speaking to the boss. He's told me he saw you and he wants to have a private talk with me so we're going out for lunch together. I'm hoping that the fact he's making it a lunch date means that I haven't screwed up too badly.'

'It's not you, Marco. Don't worry, he'll tell you all about it, I'm sure. I'm on my way out for lunch myself as a guest of the mayor, no less. I've no idea what he wants. Anyway, I have a bit of news for you. I had a visitor this morning who might be of interest in the David Berg case. Are you likely to be in the office after lunch, say around three? On second thoughts, why don't you come to my office? That way, I can tell you about the guy I saw this morning, and if you want to talk about what Virgilio has to tell you at lunchtime, we can speak freely.'

We agreed on three o'clock and I spent the rest of the short walk wondering yet again whether there was likely to be any chance of the enigmatic Mr Jacobs getting his mysterious cigar box or his three hundred thousand in gold bullion back. I had a strong suspicion that the answer was going to be no.

La Vecchia Stalla was a real Tuscan eatery. Outside, it was a fairly normal-looking building, maybe a couple of hundred years old – which was young by Florentine standards. Inside, it was noisy and crowded, with almost all the tables already occupied by people on their lunchbreak. There was a wonderful smell of grilling meat in the air and I knew that if Oscar had been with me, he would have been enchanted. I gave my name to the *padrone*, wondering how much privacy the mayor was hoping to get here with so many people potentially listening, but I needn't have worried. The restaurateur nodded and guided me to a door in the far wall marked *Privato*, behind which there was a narrow staircase leading up two floors to a small, private dining room with a single table set for two. The mayor was already there, standing by the window, looking out. He smiled when he saw me and beckoned to me. I went over to the window and we shook hands before he returned his attention to what was outside.

'Thanks for coming, Signor Armstrong. Have you ever been here before? This restaurant may be outside the *centro storico* but this private dining room – normally reserved for romantic assignations – has a wonderful view.' He pointed out across the rooftops. From here, we were looking over the green space that was the English Cemetery – in fact owned by the Swiss Evangelical Reformed Church – and on across sun-bleached terracotta roofs of all shapes and sizes to the unmistakable bulk of the Duomo capped by Brunelleschi's massive dome, with Giotto's bell tower just visible to one side of it. Over to our left was the equally impressive basilica of Santa Croce with the panoramic viewing point of Piazzale Michelangelo on the hill across the river beyond it. This was the magnificence of Florence encapsulated.

I glanced across at the mayor. 'You're right, it's a spectacular view. I love this city.'

He looked back and gave me a warm smile. 'So do I.' He indicated the table. 'And now we have to concentrate on what we're going to eat. I don't know how hungry you're feeling but they do a magnificent mixed grill here.'

I nodded enthusiastically, reflecting that if Oscar had been with me, he would also have been nodding in agreement.

'And, to simplify matters, why don't we have their mixed antipasti as a starter? You're very welcome to have a pasta course as well but, from experience, I think you'll probably find it unnecessary. The portions here are decidedly generous.'

We sat down, and only a minute or so later, a waitress appeared to take our order. There was no sign of a menu on the table and it was all done verbally. She didn't write anything down but just nodded and left us alone. The mayor and I chatted about Florence for a few minutes before she reappeared with a bottle of

Chianti, a carafe of water and a basket of bread. I felt sorry for her having to climb two flights of stairs each time, but I imagined she was used to it by now.

After she'd left, the mayor picked up the bottle and filled our glasses. 'Thank you for seeing me at such short notice, Signor Armstrong, I really appreciate it.' He took a mouthful of wine, set down his glass, and his expression became more serious. 'I need your help in a personal matter.'

That answered one question. 'I'm happy to do anything I can. Why don't you tell me all about it?'

'It's my daughter Monica. I have twin girls; they're now twenty-one, both studying at university here. Virginia, the elder by a minute and a half, is studying history, and Monica is doing drama.'

It occurred to me that Anna might even know the older twin as she was studying history, but I made no comment and let the mayor continue.

'The problem I have is that Monica appears to have found herself a new boyfriend.'

A pause ensued while I could see him trying to choose his words, so I gave him a little prompt. 'An *unsuitable* boyfriend?'

He nodded, but then did his best to clarify the situation. 'I really don't know. I fear that he's unsuitable, but the problem I have is that I've no idea who he is. She's been going out with him now since before Christmas, but she refuses to speak about him or to introduce him to us. In the past, she's had lots of boyfriends and she's always spoken freely about them, but what's worrying my wife and myself is the secrecy with this one. I fear that there has to be a reason for it.' He looked up from his wine glass. 'If you can spare the time, I'd simply like you to find out who the man is and report back to me, but above all without her knowing that

I've employed a private investigator. Is that the sort of thing you might feel able to do?'

I was quick to assure him that I'd be happy to help and pulled out my notebook. I shot a few questions at him and made some notes, starting with the fact that, although Monica was still living at home, she often spent nights away, presumably with the new boyfriend, but her parents didn't even know his name, let alone where he lived. The elder twin, Virginia, claimed to know little more than they did, although the mayor and his wife had the impression that she probably knew more than she was letting on, because there had always been a special bond between the twins. I made a note of where Monica was studying and her father gave me a rough idea of her timetable, although this appeared to change on a weekly basis. He sent me a recent photo of her and I could immediately see how she'd managed to have a regular supply of boyfriends. There was no doubt that she was a beautiful young woman.

I had just about got all the information I needed when the waitress reappeared with our antipasti.

This was about as traditional Florentine as it gets. There were slices of grilled bread, rubbed with garlic and salt, some topped with chopped tomatoes, some with chopped mushrooms or chicken liver pâté. Along with these there were slices of excellent cured ham, *finocchiona* salami flavoured with fennel, and slices of pecorino cheese. The mayor hadn't been joking about the quantity on offer; the selection of antipasti alone was a whole lot more than I would normally have eaten at lunchtime. And there was still the mixed grill to come. Oscar would have been very jealous.

We chatted over the meal and I told him about my daughter, now almost thirty-two and engaged to be married, while he told me about his two girls – of whom he was clearly very proud. I asked him about his job and he gave me an insight into how much it entailed. Apart from the complications of running a city of almost four hundred thousand people, with the eye-watering figure of many millions of visitors each year, there were all the formal receptions, investitures, and other events at which he had to be present. I asked him how he ever found time to write his novels, and he shook his head ruefully before throwing the question back at me.

'By the way, I started your book yesterday and I'm already almost halfway through and loving it. How do *you* manage to find time to write when you have a full-time job?'

I thanked him for the positive feedback and told him that I also struggled to find the time to write. He asked me if I was actively working on a new book and I told him that I'd only just started one, this time set in neighbouring Siena. I decided that I'd better go out and buy one of his books. The least I felt I should do would be to read one of his historical novels and maybe pass it on to Anna. She was the history expert in our household.

Only a few minutes after the remains of the antipasti had been cleared away, a waiter appeared carrying our mixed grill. He was a strong-looking young man and I could see why he needed the muscles. He was bearing a large silver platter, almost the size of a tray, on which there was a mountain of food. He set it down in front of us, nodded politely and left us to it. I glanced across at the mayor and saw him studying the expression on my face. He grinned.

'And it tastes as good as it looks, believe me.'

There were pork chops, chicken breasts, slabs of beef that would have been a meal in themselves, as well as Tuscan sausages, split in half down the middle and grilled inside and out. The meat was accompanied by a pile of little roast potatoes, slices of grilled aubergines and courgettes and a heap of *peperonata* – a spicy mix of onions, red, yellow and green peppers, and chopped tomatoes. I took a deep breath, picked up the serving spoons and helped myself. The mayor was right. It was outstanding.

We got talking about dogs, and the mayor – 'Call me Ugo' – asked me about the black Labrador he'd seen at the book launch. I told him about Oscar and he told me his wife had a dachshund, but I got the impression that he longed for a bigger dog. Of course, with his work commitments, he knew he wouldn't have the time to dedicate to walking it.

We were still talking about dogs when we both finally admitted defeat and threw in the towel. I had eaten enough to last me for the rest of the week and there was still meat left over. The mayor very kindly asked the waitress if she could organise a doggy bag for Oscar – he told me his dog was too spoilt to deign to eat leftovers. When this was handed to me on our way out of the restaurant, the waitress must have added even more bits of meat as it felt as if it weighed at least a kilo. Somehow, I had a feeling Oscar was going to forgive me for not taking him out to lunch.

We shook hands outside the restaurant and I thanked the mayor for the meal, promising I would see what I could find out about his daughter's boyfriend and report back as soon as possible. A shiny Mercedes was waiting by the kerb and the mayor offered me a lift back to my office, but I told him I needed the walk. In fact, after everything I'd eaten, I probably needed at least a twenty-mile route march. I watched him leave for his next appointment – opening a new sports hall in the suburb of Rifredi – and I reflected on how very human and approachable he had been. I hoped I wouldn't discover anything sinister as far as his daughter's mysterious boyfriend was concerned. He had enough on his plate already, trying to run this amazing city.

10

MONDAY AFTERNOON

On my way back to the office, I stopped off at a bookshop and bought myself a copy of *Revenge – a Medici Family Drama* by Ugo Gallo and was delighted to see a pile of my murder mysteries on display. I would definitely pass his book on to Anna to read after I'd had a go at it, and no doubt she would be able to comment on the historical accuracy of the mayor's research.

At the office, I received a warm welcome from Oscar – made even warmer when I gave him a succulent piece of steak the size of a pack of cards. I then took him for a walk and, out of curiosity, I went back to the Ponte Vecchio. The entrance to David Berg's shop was still taped shut, but as far as I could see, there were no longer any police officers inside so presumably the forensic investigations had all finished. We crossed over to the other side of the river and from there, we walked upstream to the next bridge, the Ponte alle Grazie. As we walked along, I gazed across the water at the predominantly white palazzi lining the river with the clock-tower of the Palazzo Vecchio and the cupola of the Duomo beyond. Looking back, I could see the Ponte Vecchio in all its glory, three storeys high and with three perfect open arches in the centre. It was an iconic view and I never tired of it, although the thought that only a matter of days earlier, an elderly Dutchman had been found hanging there was sobering, and my mind was once more drawn to the motivation behind that murder. Had it been robbery or something more personal?

We crossed the river again and walked past the Basilica of Santa Croce, which houses the tombs of such legendary names as Michelangelo and Galileo. History is everywhere in Florence and, after some of the stories Anna had told me about events in the Middle Ages, I knew that a random murder was as nothing when compared to some of the brutal things that had happened here over the centuries.

As I neared the office, I returned my thoughts to business and checked my watch. It was two forty-five and Marco would be coming to see me soon, so he would be able to let me know if they'd found any more clues to help with the murder investigation – although I wasn't holding my breath. I was definitely coming around to thinking that the killer must have been a pro, so it was highly unlikely that he would have been careless enough to leave any fingerprints or DNA for the police to find.

At three o'clock, Marco arrived and I was delighted to see Virgilio accompanying him. Oscar was also very pleased to see the two of them, as was Lina. Her husband was looking as if a burden had been lifted from his shoulders and the relief on her own face was plain to see. I brought the two men into my office, closed the door, and looked at them expectantly. 'Well...'

Virgilio answered first. 'I've had a long talk to Marco, and we've agreed to work together – in the greatest secrecy – to try to uncover the identity of whoever's making files disappear.'

Marco nodded in agreement. 'When the *commissario* told me of his suspicions, it immediately rang a bell with me. I've been trying to investigate the death of an asylum seeker that took place two months ago and it's as if it never happened. There's virtually nothing on the system to show that the man even existed, let alone was murdered.'

I thought back to the conversation Virgilio had had with me the previous day. 'As I understand it, two asylum seekers have been murdered in the last few months and the police records of the deaths have disappeared. From what little you know of the two men – assuming they were men – is there anything that links them together?'

Virgilio answered. 'Not a lot. For what it's worth, they were both male and, from their appearance, I would have said sub-Saharan African, with very dark skin but, like so many so-called asylum seekers, they were carrying no documents. That might be because their passports or ID documents were stolen by their killer, but quite possibly the documents had been deliberately lost or destroyed by the victims themselves. That way, they could refuse to say exactly where they'd come from.' He caught my eye and explained, although this wasn't news to me. 'It's legal to deport illegal migrants from the EU back to their home countries if they don't qualify for refugee status, but if we don't know where they come from, we don't know where to send them, so they can't be removed. Crazy, eh? They most probably arrived in southern Italy by boat via Libya and were planning on heading north to Germany or even the UK.'

'So you have no names for them?'

Virgilio shook his head. 'I've spoken to the two officers who discovered the bodies and they confirm there were no documents or personal belongings on either, nothing more than the clothes they were wearing. None of the other migrants they questioned in the station area claimed to know anything about them so, no, they were logged as *Sconosciuto 07* and *Sconosciuto 08*. As you can tell from the numbers, these weren't the first people to end up dead and unidentified this year. How do you refer to unidentified bodies in the UK?'

'Normally John Doe – don't ask me why. Were they both killed in the same way?'

'Yes. Both were stabbed with a narrow blade. Just one single stab wound in each case, direct to the heart – no fuss, no struggle, and very little blood.'

All three of us looked at each other for a moment before I stated the obvious. 'That sounds like the work of a professional to me.' I shook my head in disbelief. 'So why would somebody want to pay good money for a hitman to murder a couple of guys who'd just got off a boat from Africa? What about drugs? Any trace of illegal substances?'

Virgilio shook his head again. 'Nothing. From the way they were dressed, neither man can have had much in the way of money, so I can't imagine that robbery could be the motive. Why would anybody run the risk of going to jail for a long time by stabbing somebody for the sake of a few euros? No, there must be another reason.'

Marco hazarded a guess. 'Could it be some sort of rogue vigilante with a grudge against asylum seekers or people of colour?'

Virgilio nodded. 'Anything's possible. The first problem, though, is to find out why somebody on the force is deleting the files. Presumably, it's so as to remove evidence and protect the killer.'

I added the obvious corollary. 'Unless the person removing the evidence *is* the killer.' I saw Marco and Virgilio look at each other in horror at the thought of a fellow officer killing people, so I decided it best to move the conversation on. 'While I remember, Marco, let me tell you about the man who came to see me this morning.' I wasn't worried about the old Dutchman's threats if I revealed what he had said – I had been threatened by far more dangerous people over the years. I told them everything that I'd heard from Axel Jacobs, particularly his conviction that Berg's murder had been robbery, possibly to the tune of three hundred thousand euros, and Marco whistled in awe.

'Three hundred thousand, that's not chicken feed. I wouldn't like to be in this man Jacobs's shoes. If we open the safe in Berg's villa and find that Jacobs's cigar box isn't there, he's three hundred thousand out of pocket. If it is there, he's going to find himself fighting an uphill battle to prove that the stuff belongs to him and not Berg. Either way, I don't envy him.'

'Talking of Berg's safe, what about his will? Have you been able to talk to his lawyer yet?'

Marco's face darkened. 'Yes, I managed to speak to him just before lunch, but I didn't get much out of him – not that he was uncooperative. He had very little to tell. As we've already worked out for ourselves, he told me that Berg didn't trust anybody, and that included him. On the Wednesday before the old man's death, they met up and talked for an hour, mainly about a change in European regulations regarding dealings in precious metals and precious stones. In the course of the conversation, Berg referred briefly to his will, indicating that the housekeeper and her husband had witnessed it, but he didn't disclose its contents. So, yes, he appears to have a will, but it remains to be seen who the beneficiaries are.'

I shared his frustration. Looking across at Virgilio, I changed to the other subject again. 'As far as the mystery of the missing files is concerned, later on this afternoon, I'm going to go and check out the houses of the three police officer suspects and I'll see if I can find anybody who can give me any information.'

He nodded but added a caveat. 'Thanks, Dan, but do remember to keep it low-key. At the moment, these are just possibles, not real, solid suspects, and if word were to get back to them that they were under suspicion, there would be all hell to pay.'

'Believe me, Virgilio, I'll be careful. I just want to get an idea of what sort of people they are outside the work environment. Presumably, you guys will be doing your best to look for the missing files from inside the force and, even better, trying to find out who wiped them. Good luck with that.' I turned my attention to Marco. 'What about the Ponte Vecchio case? Have the Swiss told you when their technician will be arriving?'

He shrugged his shoulders. 'Still waiting to hear. I have a feeling the contents of that safe are going to be crucial to cracking this case and it's frustrating having to wait.'

'What about Berg's family? I imagine you've done background checks on them. Find anything?'

'Nothing significant. None of them has a criminal record. I was rather hoping that we might uncover something suspicious about Guido, the daughter's boyfriend, but he would appear to be squeaky clean – and loaded. He comes from a very wealthy family in Randstad, halfway between Amsterdam and The Hague, and, before you ask, they're tulip farmers on a vast scale, nothing to do with jewellery.'

'And Luuc? I thought he looked the least sympathetic.'

'Not even a parking fine. He's clean.'

'Pity. And are they all still staying at the victim's house?'

'I've asked them to stay at least until the safe gets opened, and they seem quite willing – no doubt they're hoping to find the old man's will in there. To what extent it's in their favour remains to be seen.'

I reflected that we didn't appear to be getting anywhere fast in this case. It certainly wasn't as if we had suspects piling up.

* * *

Once Virgilio and Marco had left, I set off with Oscar to check out the homes of the two more senior officers that were both within easy walking distance of my office. I started with Giuseppe Verdi, the *vice questore*. His apartment was situated in a three-storey building less than five minutes' walk from my office, backing onto the *Giardino della Gherardesca* – yet another beautiful green space in the middle of Florence, which is off limits to the general public, unless they happen to be guests of the exclusive five-star Four Seasons Hotel that now owns it. The front door of Verdi's three-or-four-hundred-year-old building was a historical treasure in itself, made of beautifully carved, highly polished wood and set in a sculpted stone surround. A surreptitious glance at the brass bell-pushes on the panel beside it told me that there were only four apartments in the building and the *vice questore* occupied the top-floor flat.

I walked on along the road for fifty yards before crossing and stopping, ostensibly so that Oscar could sniff and mark one of the trees flanking the pavement. Taking care not to appear too obvious, I turned my head so that I was able to look back towards the *vice questore*'s building and it was immediately clear that his apartment enjoyed its own rooftop terrace. I had no doubt that the views from up there over the ornamental gardens and back across the city must be spectacular. He was a lucky man and, in order to be able to afford to live in a place like this, he also had to be a wealthy man. I wondered how much the salary of the second-in-command of the Florence police force might be. No doubt this was a generous amount, but would it be enough to support a lifestyle like this without some additional subsidy – like donations from a murderer keen to cover his back, for example?

There was nobody about, no nearby corner shop or bar where I could casually enquire about the man who owned the top-floor flat, so in the end, all I could do was to move on to the next address. This was the home of Vincenzo Grande, the Sicilian superintendent, and it was about twenty minutes' walk away, on the far side of the main station. Although just inside the *centro storico*, this building was situated on one of a number of roads running through the town centre for the exclusive use of public services, buses, taxis and so on as well as pedestrians. In consequence, it was far less peaceful than Giuseppe Verdi's place, although still only a convenient ten-minute walk from the police station itself. This was a bigger building than Verdi's and from the doorbells, I worked out that it housed a dozen or so apartments. It looked as though Grande lived on the first or second floor, certainly not the penthouse. A good address, but not overly opulent.

From an investigative point of view, this place was preferable because there was a bar at street level, and it was possible that this was frequented by the superintendent himself. I went in, ordered an espresso and struck up a conversation with the chatty barista. I remembered Grande's hobby of hunting and used that as an intro, adding that one of my friends lived close by who was an avid hunter. The barman immediately guessed to whom I was referring. 'You must mean Vincenzo. He lives in this building a couple of floors above us. He often comes in for a coffee and he's always talking about hunting.'

I felt sure it had to be Grande, but I shook my head, distancing myself from the superintendent just in case the friendly barman were to inform him next time he saw him that a man with a black dog had claimed to know him.

'No, my friend lives about a hundred metres further down that way.' I pointed vaguely along the road. 'Do you hunt?'

'When I get the chance, but I spend most of my life here behind the counter. What about you? Do you hunt?'

'Back home in Ireland.' No harm in adding a bit more disinformation. 'I'm here on holiday for a couple of weeks.' I pointed at Oscar. 'I'm staying with friends on the other side of the river and I told them I'd give the dog a walk. What about your man who lives here? Where does he go for his hunting?'

'Vincenzo? He was telling me he went hunting wild boar down in the hills of southern Tuscany last autumn, but I think he spends most of his free time nowadays at the lake.' In answer to my enquiring look, he explained. 'It's not far from the airport, out to the west of Florence in the valley of the Arno. There are two or three lakes there surrounded by reeds and they regularly get ducks and geese coming in.' He leant towards me and lowered his voice to a conspiratorial whisper. 'Mind you, from what he tells me, that's not all you get there.'

'Such as?'

'They have a clubhouse and a cook, but they also have bedrooms, if you know what I mean.' He grinned at me and tapped the side of his nose with a finger. 'You don't so much rent the room as the company inside it, female company, and I'm not talking about other hunters.'

This didn't come as a total surprise. As well as food, wine, cars, football and hunting, I'm sure many Italian men would also include women in their list of hobbies. *I'm going hunting, dear*, would be a convenient way of slipping out of the house for a bit of hanky-panky without fear of most wives wanting to tag along. Maybe Vincenzo Grande's Achilles heel was a penchant for illicit sex. Given that he was a senior police officer, this could make him open to blackmail. Could it be that in return for silence as far as his extramarital activities were concerned, Grande had agreed to make some incriminating police files disappear?

From there, I returned to the office, checked with Lina that nothing new had come in, and picked up my van. I drove out of town in the direction of Virgilio's house in the suburbs and found

Inspector Roberto Faldo's house in a new development about a kilometre or so from there. His was the end property on a small development of a dozen modern, two-storey houses and it looked stylish and well-constructed. There was a new Mini on the drive and the front garden was well maintained. I wondered if he was renting or if he had bought it. Within easy reach of central Florence, it wouldn't have come cheap. I presumed his wife also worked because they were most probably faced with a hefty rental bill or mortgage repayment each month. This didn't necessarily make him more suspicious, but I put a mental asterisk alongside his name in my head all the same.

Unfortunately, out here in the suburbs, there were no convenient local bars or shops and, apart from a lone woman walking her poodle, there was nobody to be seen. Presumably, most of the people who lived here were still working at their jobs in the city. I took one final look and then drove up to the end of the road to turn around. As far as I could see from this cursory look, Roberto Faldo was living within his means – but probably only just.

As I set off for home, I reviewed the three men in my head and provisionally rated their possible culpability, assigning first place to Vice Questore Verdi, while Superintendent Grande and Inspector Faldo shared second place, but that could all change so easily.

11

TUESDAY MORNING

I went into the office earlier than usual next morning and spent the time between eight and nine on the computer checking, among other things, to see if there was anything there about Axel Jacobs, dealer in precious stones and metals. There were a number of entries in Dutch, but I also found a couple in English that confirmed what he'd told me. By the look of it, he was a reputable trader, although what he'd said about his 'gentleman's agreement' with David Berg rather threw that into question. There were a few photos of him at trade fairs and what looked like a diamond dealers' conference, and they confirmed that he was who he said he was. As far as helping him get hold of his cigar box containing three hundred thousand euros' worth of precious stones or metals – or both – was concerned, I had very few options. It was quite clear that until the safe at Berg's villa could be opened, there was no way of knowing if Jacob's property was there or not, and if it wasn't, he would face an uphill struggle to get it back. At least the contents of the safe might help us work out who might have killed Berg and stolen the goods.

At nine o'clock, Lina arrived, looking more relaxed than the previous day. The fact that Virgilio had decided to share his concerns with Marco and me must have had a beneficial effect on him and, by extension, on his wife. I made her a cup of coffee and Oscar gave her a warm welcome. By the time I went back into my office, she was looking more like her normal self. Remembering my other case, I spent half an hour trawling the Internet for anything that might shed light on Monica Gallo, the mayor's daughter. She had various social media accounts with the usual birthday celebrations, holiday snaps, and pictures of her in a number of drama productions, but there was no sign of a boyfriend – at least not for several years. In case Anna might know Virginia, the other twin, in the history department, I gave her a call and a ray of hope appeared.

'Virginia Gallo, yes, I know her. She's a good student, works hard and always hands in her work on time. As for her sister, Monica, I sometimes see them together and, as you can imagine, two identical, good-looking girls like that are never short of admiring – or predatory – males circling around them, but I'm not aware of anybody special for either of them. I'll have a word with my colleagues. I know one of the drama teachers very well, and she might be able to tell me more about Monica. Watch this space.'

By the time I set off in the van for my meeting with the mysterious Zebra in the Bar Sport in Via del Fondo, I was none the wiser about Monica's 'unsuitable' boyfriend, and I spent the short journey turning over in my head how I should proceed. In the end, I decided to wait until I'd heard back from Anna.

Via del Fondo looked as though it had seen better days. The café where I was meeting Zebra was on the corner, right at the beginning of the road, and it looked decidedly dodgy – the sort of place where you pay cash, keep your hands on your wallet, and find a seat with your back to the wall, not too far from the way out. The road surface was pitted with potholes and there was a burnt-out car rusting at the side of the road. A row of decrepit terraced houses at the far end had been taped off, and there were notices everywhere warning people to stay away as the properties were earmarked for demolition. This was a far cry from the splendour of Piazza del Duomo and no doubt far, far off the tourist trail. As I was early for my appointment, I drove past the café and bumped slowly along the rough road until I reached the end and found the theatre. This looked little better than the surrounding houses although, in fairness, there was no demolition notice to be seen. The name of the theatre had been painted onto a long canvas banner, which hung rather pathetically over what had no doubt once been the entrance to an old factory. One thing was for sure – it certainly didn't look like Broadway.

I turned back and parked outside the café, hoping that I would find the wheels still attached to the vehicle when I returned to it. It was that kind of place. The only people I saw as I climbed out of the van were a couple of what the Italians refer to as *extracomunitari* – literally from outside the European Union. Mind you, I reminded myself, since Brexit, I was also an *extracomunitario*, although probably not in such dire straits as these guys. The idea of having to leave their homes and families thousands of kilometres away and make the perilous journey across the Mediterranean in the hope of finding a better life was both daunting and potentially dangerous – as the two John Does murdered at the station proved only too graphically. For a moment, I wondered how I would have fared under such circumstances and, as always, I felt a pang of sympathy for them. Even so, I made sure I left nothing visible inside the van and locked it securely before heading for the door of the café.

The interior of the café lived up to my low expectations. In fairness, it looked clean, but there were three or four different types of chairs to be seen at the equally mismatched tables, and the clientele was uninspiring – well, most of them. There were three old men sitting in there and a suspicious smell of tobacco in the air – even though smoking in bars and restaurants has been banned in Italy for quite a few years now. The barman was wearing a blotchy, grey T-shirt, which might have started life white and had probably fitted him twenty years earlier but now was fighting a losing battle against his expanding waistline. He had a shaved head and one of the bushiest moustaches I had ever seen. Fortunately, Oscar was more interested in sniffing whatever the floor smelled of and didn't look up. If he'd seen the luxuriant moustache, he would probably have mistaken it for a squirrel.

However, in the midst of this somewhat depressing scene, there was one very bright exception. I don't know what I'd been expecting from a person called Zebra – all right, not four legs and black and white stripes – but I was unprepared for the vision before me. Zebra was a woman, but I had no idea how old she was. She certainly wouldn't see thirty again, and she might even have been as old as me. At a guess – and it was only a guess – I put her down as in her late forties. Her hair was amazingly long, hanging right down to her waist, and I counted at least ten different colours in the stripes that ran all the way up to her scalp. Her eyes were so heavily made up, she looked more like a panda than a zebra, but her face was friendly and her eyes sparkled mischievously.

Oscar's reaction to Zebra was remarkable, even for him. The moment he clapped eyes on her, he positively bounded across the floor towards her and, without hesitating, jumped athletically onto her lap, where he proceeded to lick her face. I hurried over to haul him off her, but she held up a restraining hand.

'Don't worry, he's fine. What a beautiful dog!' She then returned her attention to my clearly smitten Labrador. 'Who's a good boy? You are, aren't you? Yes, you are.' She enveloped him in a hug that virtually hid him from sight. She wasn't a small woman and she was wearing a voluminous, kaftan-like robe in a mixture of primary colours that effectively swallowed Oscar up. I had to wait a good half a minute before his head reappeared, tongue hanging out, grinning from ear to ear. Zebra cradled him in her arms as she looked across at me.

'I presume you are Signor Armstrong.' She was using the familiar form of the pronoun 'you'.

'I am indeed, and you must be Signora Zebra.'

'Just Zebra. I'm the director of the Teatro dell'Arno.' She disentangled her right arm from the happy dog and held out her hand towards me. There was at least one ring on every finger and there were so many bracelets on her wrist, I felt sure she needed strong arm muscles to lift them and probably jingled as she walked down the street. I shook her hand and got down to business.

'How can I help?'

'Stuff has started to go missing. I mean, it's been stolen. Not very expensive stuff – we don't really have anything like that there – but money from purses and wallets, a couple of silk scarves and my old iPad. I know it doesn't sound like much, but none of us can afford to lose out like that. It's so mean.'

'Can I ask why you haven't reported this to the police – or have you?'

She shook her head. 'No. If I involve the police, I know what'll happen. If they can be bothered to come out – and there's no guarantee – they'll say the stuff's been stolen by one of the asylum seekers who live around here and they might even arrest all of them or move them on. I wouldn't like that on my conscience.'

'The asylum seekers are living in those houses that are going to be demolished?'

'Yes, poor things. God only knows what they'll do when that happens. They have nowhere to go.'

'You don't think the asylum seekers are responsible?' Given their shortage of money, it seemed a realistic possibility.

Zebra shook her head. 'They wouldn't steal from us. I know it.'

She didn't appear to have any doubts, but I wasn't so sure. Still, setting aside my suspicions for now, I continued. 'If it's not one of the asylum seekers, who do you think it might be? I imagine quite a few people come in and out of the theatre every day. Could it be one of your actors, your other staff, cleaners or just somebody else who wanders in from the outside?'

She shrugged. 'I can't imagine for a moment that it could be one of our people but, you're right, anybody can walk in if they like; security is very lax.' She stopped and corrected herself. 'Or rather, security is non-existent. We can't afford any.'

I took a good look at her as she stroked Oscar, who had rolled over onto his back on her lap with all four paws in the air, tail wagging, a blissful expression on his face, and I made a decision. 'I'm sure you're aware that I normally charge for my time, but I'd like to help you. I did a bit of acting at school a long time ago and I feel sorry you're having to go through this. The fact is that I don't think there's a lot I'm going to be able to do for you. I don't have access to police files to check for any previous offenders and, besides, there's no guarantee it's the same person doing all the stealing. There could be different people wandering in and out and helping themselves. What I would suggest is that I come with you now to the theatre, take a look around, and see if I can think of anything that might help – prevention rather than cure. I won't make any charge for that. I'd rather you saved your money for your shows.'

She reached across the table with her free hand and caught

hold of one of mine. 'You're a good man, Signor Armstrong. Thank you most warmly. You're right, we need every cent just to keep the lights on.'

She eased a reluctant Oscar off her lap and down onto the floor again. When she stood up, I saw that she was almost as tall as I was and quite a lot broader in the beam. Woe betide any sneak thief that she caught.

We emerged from the café into the relatively fresher air of the street. The theatre was only a couple of hundred metres away from here and normally, I would have just left the van where it was and walked, but, because of the kind of down-at-heel area this was, we climbed in and I drove along to the theatre, parking as close to the entrance as possible. I turned off the engine and glanced sideways at Zebra.

'The fact that you chose to meet me in the café, was that because you do suspect it might be somebody on your staff or among the actors after all? Were you trying to keep my identity secret from them?'

She hesitated and then nodded reluctantly. 'Yes, I suppose that's what I was trying to do, although I still find it hard to believe that one of our people might be behind these thefts. But, of course, now they're going to see you, and I'll just have to tell them who you are.'

'I know this will be a difficult question for you, but now that it appears that you might have your doubts about your actors or staff, is there anybody you consider to be suspicious? Is there anybody you've mentally earmarked as a possible thief?'

'We don't have many staff. We have a technician who does everything from lighting the performances to fixing the toilets when they overflow. There's our PR manager, who also doubles as our accountant and ticket seller, and there are a couple of part-time cleaners. I suppose it's just possible that one of the cleaners might be the culprit, but it feels so awful even to be considering it.'

'Are all four staff members here at the moment?'

'Yes. We have a dress rehearsal later today for our next production, which opens on Saturday, and we're doing our best to get everything ready. I hope you being here doesn't spoil the atmosphere.'

I thought quickly. 'There's no need to tell them that I'm a private investigator. If anybody asks what I'm doing wandering about, tell them I'm your long-lost cousin Dan from England, here for a few days, and you're just showing me around. How does that sound?'

She smiled happily. 'That sounds like an excellent idea, Signor Armstrong.'

I smiled back and shook my head. 'No, not Signor Armstrong. I'm Cousin Dan, remember?'

'Of course. Welcome, Cousin Dan. By the way, how very rude of me – I haven't been formally introduced to your furry friend.'

'He's Oscar and he's very pleased to meet you, Zebra.'

I spent half an hour wandering around the interior of the theatre, surreptitiously scribbling in my notebook. I had quite enjoyed drama class when I was at school and getting behind the scenes in a theatre – albeit a far from wealthy one – was fascinating. Backstage, there were piles of pretty obviously scavenged timber and a roll of canvas, no doubt used for making scenery. Behind the stage was a wardrobe room that smelt not unlike the changing rooms in the police gym, and I noticed that even Oscar didn't stick around in there for long.

I met gangly Dario, the jack-of-all-trades technician, and Camilla, the accountant who was also responsible for PR. I couldn't help smiling when I was introduced to her. Apart from the name, she couldn't have been any more different from the current Queen of England. She was tiny, stick thin, and one of those people who appear so nervous, they rarely dare to look up from their shoes. Somehow, however, I couldn't see this as a sign of guilt and I mentally dismissed both her and Dario from the list of likely suspects.

This left me with the actors, but they wouldn't turn up until later on, and the two cleaners, both black women. Their reaction to seeing Oscar was initially one of mistrust until he wandered across, tail wagging, and soon won them over. They appeared to be doing a very industrious job, but communication with them was extremely difficult – at first. Neither spoke more than a few words of Italian, and Zebra had to introduce me as Cousin Dan in halting, broken French. To my surprise, when the older of the two women heard me described as the cousin from England, she switched to fluent English.

'My sister lives in England and that's where we're headed. She's been living in London for the past five years and she says it's a wonderful place.'

Probably because of my former job, I don't look on Britain's capital city through the same rose-tinted glasses, but it was good to hear somebody singing the country's praises for once. I complimented her on her English and she told me she'd been a teacher of English in the north of the Central African Republic until she and her husband had had to flee the country, one step ahead of a band of vicious militia fighters. She introduced me to the woman alongside her as Vanda, her sister-in-law, and introduced herself as Amélie. She told me her husband was currently working on a building site not far from the theatre while she and Vanda worked here until they could get together enough money to continue their journey north. She was charming, articulate and I really couldn't see her stealing a packet of cigarettes from anybody. Her sister-in-law, on the other hand, had a more furtive look about her, but that might just have been natural shyness.

Finally, I sat down with Zebra again and gave her my list of recommendations. These were mostly practical: put bolts on all outside doors and keep them locked, don't leave stuff lying around, earmark one room for more valuable things and keep it locked as well. As far as the common area where most of the thefts had taken place was concerned, I offered her the loan of a motion sensor camera for a week or two and she accepted the offer gratefully. I told her I'd drop it around and set it up for her later in the day, and then it was time for me to leave. I shook her hand, wished her well, and dragged my reluctant dog away from his new best – and very colourful – friend.

On the way back to the office, I discussed with Oscar why I was being so kind to Zebra when I had so much other stuff to occupy me. Maybe it was because Oscar clearly thought she was the best thing since sliced bread – or, in his case, any food – or maybe it was a nostalgic nod to my days of amateur dramatics at school all those years ago. Of course, I suggested to him as I picked my way through the traffic, maybe it was just because I was a nice guy.

The only response from him was a cavernous sigh and a thud as he settled down for a quick nap.

12

TUESDAY AFTERNOON

I met up with Anna for a snack lunch in a little café near the university. As usual, she opted for a goat's cheese and aubergine focaccia sandwich while I had a plate of mixed bruschetta, with a couple of biscuits for my ever-hungry dog. As we ate, she told me that she had spoken to her friend, Francesca, in the drama department, about Monica Gallo, the mayor's daughter.

'Francesca is actually Monica's tutor so she knows her pretty well. She says Monica's a good, motivated student who has a real love of acting. In fact, according to Francesca, if she has a weakness, it's that she spends so much time doing amateur dramatics that she sometimes gets behind in her coursework. But, overall, she's a good student. As for boyfriends, Francesca didn't know of anybody special but, just like her sister, there's no shortage of men hanging around her.'

I gave a lot of thought to my next step. I could wander around the drama department of the university pretending to be a mature student, but if Monica's tutor wasn't aware of the identity of the mysterious boyfriend – always assuming there was one – then I could hardly expect to find that out in an afternoon.

Besides which, from what the mayor had said, Monica didn't have classes on Tuesday afternoons so she was unlikely to be there. I decided to sleep on it tonight and then pay a visit to the drama department next morning.

After lunch, I went back to the office, gave Oscar his food and picked up a spy camera with a motion sensor before heading back to the Teatro dell'Arno. This time, I found four cars parked outside the theatre along with a handful of bikes and scooters. Inside, the scene was very different from this morning. The lights were on in the auditorium and there were half a dozen actors on stage. Sitting in the front row with a clipboard and a pen, no doubt observing the performance closely, was Zebra. I didn't want to interrupt what was obviously the dress rehearsal for their new play, so I sat down a few rows back, hanging onto Oscar's collar in case he spotted his new best friend and decided to make a dash for her. From the costumes, it looked as if the play was set here in Italy just before or during the Second World War. It was well over a minute before I suddenly realised that I recognised the face of the actor playing the lead female role. It was none other than Monica Gallo, the mayor's daughter.

I sat and watched for almost half an hour, interested in the play – which I still couldn't identify – and fascinated by Monica. Apart from being stunningly attractive, she had a lovely clear voice, and I was able to follow almost all of her dialogue while with some of the other actors, I struggled. It was obviously a very tense and dramatic production and she was most convincing in her desperation towards her boyfriend or husband, played by a tall, good-looking man with an enviable head of glossy, chestnut-brown hair and a commanding presence onstage. There were only three other actors on stage most of the time: a middle-aged woman who looked like a traditional housewife, a younger man in the uniform of one of Mussolini's blackshirts, and a man wearing faded overalls and a white T-shirt. This man was probably still in his twenties but he had been made up to look older – in my view, not completely convincingly. He didn't have many lines to say, which was probably just as well as I somehow got the feeling he wasn't concentrating as hard as he should have been – but what did I know about directing a play?

Finally, the act ended and the curtains were closed. The actors disappeared and Zebra stood up. I felt tempted to clap but then decided against it as there were only two of us in the audience. As it was, Zebra turned, spotted me, and beckoned.

Oscar interpreted the invitation as being for him and he got there first, tail wagging enthusiastically. She crouched down and made a real fuss of him, to which he responded enthusiastically.

I waited until she straightened up again before indicating the bag in my hand. I kept my voice low although we were now alone. '*Ciao*, Zebra. I've brought the camera. If you've got a moment, I'll set it up for you.'

She led me back to the small room that she used as an office, where I closed the door behind us and explained how to operate the camera, linking it to her phone. I told her I didn't need it for a week or two and wished her luck. We decided to install it in the common area used by staff and actors alike and she came with me to watch as I set this up, hiding it among a pile of dusty cardboard boxes. She then offered me a cup of Nescafé, which I accepted, not so much because I wanted another coffee, but because it gave me an opportunity to do a bit of probing into the actors I'd just seen – one in particular.

I started off cautiously. 'It looks to me as though the play's set during the fascist period here in Italy, but I'm afraid my knowledge of twentieth-century drama isn't that great. What's it called and who's it by?'

'The play is called *Ultimatum* and it makes a change from the series of Shakespearean tragedies we've been doing over the winter.'

'That's a new one on me. Who wrote it?'

She looked up and caught my eye. 'I did.'

'Wow, you're a playwright as well as a theatre director. How do you find the time? I do a bit of writing myself and I struggle to fit it in with my day job.' I moved the conversation closer to my person of interest. 'I thought the woman playing the main female role was excellent. Are they really just amateurs?'

She nodded. 'They all are. They just do it for the love of the theatre. You're right, Monica is very talented. She's playing Linda, the wife of the main protagonist, and she really brings something to every role she plays.'

I did my best to sound only casually interested. 'What does she do when she's not performing?'

'She's a student. She's doing drama and I'm hoping very much to get a friend of mine to come along to the first night to see her in action. He's retired now, but he used to be a theatrical agent and if he likes her, he might be able to put her onto an agent of her own. Like I say, she's very talented and I could see her going far.'

'What about the other actors?'

'They're all good but they're not quite in her league apart from Tiberio, who has the male lead. He's a very talented actor as well, and the others do a great job apart from Paolo – he's the one in the overalls and the white T-shirt. He keeps forgetting his lines and it's not as if he has many of them to learn.' There was frustration in her voice. 'I'm afraid he isn't as dedicated as the others. It's pretty clear he hasn't been giving time to learning his lines properly, but I don't have much choice. The fact is that we've been struggling to find actors willing to give up their time in return for very little – well, nothing, really. We can't afford to pay them – not even expenses – and our audiences are never huge. It's this area, I'm afraid. The council has earmarked it for redevelopment and it's been going steadily downhill for ages.' She met my eye and shrugged. 'I have to make do with the actors I can find and I'm just lucky to have some excellent ones among them.'

I was pleased that my impression of Paolo with the scruffy overalls as being distracted had been confirmed by the director. Maybe I knew more about this business than I had thought. 'Shame he's not so motivated. He's a good-looking guy. Are he and Monica an item?' I tried to sound as casual as possible.

She shook her head and smiled. 'No, she's already taken. Besides, Paolo is more interested in members of his own sex.'

'Is Monica's partner an actor as well?'

'Yes, Tiberio, the male lead, and like I say, he's an excellent actor. He really owns the stage; you must have noticed.'

'I definitely did. I wonder how he'll react if Monica gets snapped up by an agent and shipped off to Hollywood one of these days.'

'I wouldn't be surprised if he followed her to Hollywood. Besides, if he doesn't make it as an actor, he can always work as a doctor. I'm sure he could find a good job over there.'

'He's a doctor? Wow, it must be hard for him to find the time to rehearse.'

'He's in his final year of medicine at university here and he keeps telling me it's getting more and more difficult for him to balance the two.'

I sat back and reflected on what I'd just heard, hoping that this information would satisfy the mayor that his daughter's boyfriend wasn't a waste of space. Tall, good-looking, and training to be a doctor, as well as being a talented actor, surely made him quite a catch – not least as he shared his name with the Roman Emperor Tiberius. I wondered yet again why Monica was insisting on keeping him away from her parents. Anyway, the good news as far as I was concerned was that I had quite fortuitously concluded my mission and I wouldn't need to waste hours wandering around the university next morning.

Zebra told me that she had to get back to observe the second act so I finished my coffee, persuaded my dog to relinquish the new love of his life and went back outside. The van was still there with all four wheels still attached, which was a relief. I looked at my watch. It was barely three o'clock so I called Lina to check that there was nothing urgent waiting for me back at the office and decided that, as I was on the right side of town, I'd take a trip out to Vincenzo Grande's duck shoot, just in case I might be able to find out a bit more about the man. This would also give me the opportunity to go for a good walk with Oscar.

My satnav guided me to the Zona Sportiva dei Laghi – the lakes sporting area. This was about twenty minutes to the west of Florence in the valley of the River Arno. The terrain was pan flat and almost deserted. Apart from a handful of houses along the narrow, winding access road through reed beds and fields, I hardly saw any signs of civilisation until I reached a turn-off to the right onto a rough track. A series of wooden arrows attached to a post indicated that this was home to a number of different sports clubs. I saw signs to a fishing lake, the wildfowl lake, an off-road driving club, a clay-pigeon shoot and, unexpectedly, a castle. Considering that castles were normally built on hills, finding one down here was unexpected. I left the van just off the road and decided to recce on foot with Oscar.

It was another warm day and I wished I'd changed into my shorts. There wasn't a breath of wind and I was perspiring by the time I reached the wildfowl lake. At the lakeside was a long, low, wooden building with an open terrace at the front and a sign pinned to the wall indicating that this was a bar as well as a shooting club. I saw two elderly men sitting at a table on the terrace, drinking wine. The idea of a cold beer had considerable attraction, so I made my way across to them. One of the men gave me a lazy wave and pointed at Oscar.

'Does he work?'

To the best of my knowledge, Oscar has never done a day's work in his life but, given my surroundings, I realised what the man was asking, so I shook my head and assumed an expression of exaggerated disappointment.

'No, he's just a house dog, I'm afraid. He belongs to my sister and he's never had any gun-dog training. I'm just walking him. Are you looking for a retriever?'

'Yes, indeed. It's the close season now, but when September comes along, we're going to need another one. Zorro is getting too old.' He pointed with his thumb towards what I had taken for a pile of old sacks against the wall of the building and realised that it was, in fact, a sleeping dog – from the look of it, a Labrador crossed with a haystack. As I spotted the dog, so did Oscar, and his tail started wagging. He wandered over, and Zorro managed to summon the energy to raise his head and thump his tail on the ground a couple of times before subsiding into sleep once more. Oscar gave him a good sniff before deciding to let sleeping dogs lie and he returned to my side. I indicated a table near the two men.

'Is this place members only or can I get a drink? I'm dying for a cold beer.'

The other man stood up and headed for the door. 'You take a seat. I'll bring it to you.'

A cold bottle of beer duly arrived and I took a refreshing mouthful before striking up a conversation with the two elderly gentlemen. It transpired that the club also offered clay-pigeon shooting outside the official hunting season and I was delighted to hear one of the men mention the name of the club champion.

'Vincenzo wins all the competitions. He has reactions like a cat.'

Oscar opened one eye when he heard the C word – although in Italian, it begins with a G – checked the vicinity for any of his sworn enemies and then stretched out again.

I was wondering how to find out whether the Vincenzo in question was Superintendent Grande when the answer was provided for me. 'But it's not fair; after all, he's a police officer, so he gets far more practice than the rest of us.'

I seriously doubted whether the Florence police shooting range included the use of shotguns but I kept silent on that and asked them about the facilities of the club, hoping to get confirmation of what the barista in Florence had told me. After telling me how good the chef was and how the pool table had a serious slope to the left, the smaller of the two men gave me a lascivious wink and dropped an unambiguous hint. 'And, for those who want it, there are other benefits.' Like the barista back in Florence, he tapped the side of his nose and indicated the far end of the building. 'At the weekends, there are a couple of rooms down there if you're looking for female company, if you know what I mean.'

I jumped at the opportunity he'd given me. 'Maybe the ladies down there are the secret of why your friend Vincenzo has such good reactions.'

Both men chuckled and the taller one replied. 'I hadn't thought of that. We'll have to see that he's banned from those rooms in future.'

I asked him where I would find the castle and he pointed over to the other side of the lake. 'There's not much of it left now. All of this area has been quarried for sand and gravel since the

Middle Ages and I'm sure over the years, people have helped themselves to stones from the tumbledown walls of the castle as well. There's just the tower left now.'

After paying for my beer, I left them to their wine and Zorro to his repose and set off around the lake, passing a number of pits left over from the days of the quarry. Some of these, along with heaps of earth, were clearly part of a track for the off-road club and I spotted what was presumably their clubhouse a bit further on in the largest of the quarries, with half a dozen dusty 4 x 4s parked outside. We finally reached the remains of the castle, where I sat down on a pile of stones in the shade of the dilapidated stone tower and called Marco to ask if the Swiss safe cracker had arrived yet. There was no reply so I called Virgilio and he sounded pleased to hear from me.

'*Ciao*, Dan, how's things?'

I gave him my report. 'As far as the three police officers you suspect are concerned, nothing much to report. Superintendent Grande goes duck hunting in a place where there are also hookers available – I'm there at the moment and that's been confirmed as a fact. If he's been indulging, I suppose that could make him open to blackmail and so vulnerable to being forced to interfere with police records. Inspector Faldo lives in a smart house and might be up against it as far as money is concerned so, again, that might be a cause for a bit of moonlighting, but I don't really see him or Grande as being the main suspects. For my money, the number-one suspect – but I have nothing definite against him and it's just a hunch really – is the *vice questore*, Giuseppe Verdi. I don't know if you're familiar with his house, but it's in a fabulous position and I wonder whether he might or might not be living beyond his means. If I could get hold of his bank records, it would be interesting to see if he's been receiving sums of money over and above his salary, but I suppose there's no chance of that happening at this stage. Any joy your end?'

'Thanks for doing that, Dan, and you're right about the bank accounts. Until we can catch one of them in flagrante, there's no way I can ask for their bank records without an unholy row blowing up. I've discovered nothing more. I've just tried calling Marco to see how he's getting on, but it went to the answerphone. He went off home earlier so he could spend a couple of hours digging around in the personnel files without being observed, in an attempt to see if he could unearth anything about our three suspects. I expected him back by now but until he starts answering his phone, I don't have any news. I'll let you know if anything interesting comes up.'

'Have you been following the David Berg case? I was wondering if the company from Switzerland have sent their technician to open the safe at Berg's villa yet.'

'I've just been reading up about the case now, but I can't give you an answer to that yet. I imagine Marco will know, and I'll ask him just as soon as I can speak to him. I tend to agree with him that it's looking like aggravated robbery, but I suppose it might be a family affair. A lot will depend on the terms of the old man's will. Thank you, by the way, for acting as interpreter for Marco at Berg's house on Sunday. How did the family strike you?'

'Nothing out of the ordinary. They're obviously shocked but, after thirty years of separation, they naturally enough don't seem particularly disturbed by the old man's death. They came here because of a possible inheritance and, like you say, until they see the will, I can't see how it would have been to their advantage to murder him.'

'Hang on a minute, Dan, I've got another call coming through.' I waited for no more than a minute before I heard Virgilio's voice again, now sounding stunned. 'Marco's been involved in an accident and they're taking him to hospital as we speak.'

'Wow, what sort of accident?'

'He was found lying in the road by a passer-by. Looks like a hit and run and he's badly injured.'

My mind was racing. Could it be that this hadn't been a simple accident? After all, Virgilio had just told me that Marco had been trawling through the files of the three suspects. Might this mean that one of them was guilty, not only of removing the missing files, but now of attempting to murder a fellow officer in order to stop him getting too close?

'How is Marco? How serious is it?'

'They say it looks bad, but for now, all I know is that he's still alive and on his way to hospital. I'm going to go there straight away.'

'I'm out in the country with Oscar at the moment. Would you give me a call as soon as you know how he is? Are you thinking what I'm thinking?'

His voice when he replied was grim. 'Was it really an accident?'

13

TUESDAY EVENING

The call from Virgilio didn't come through until gone six, by which time I was back in the office, checking up on the Berg family on the Internet, but without discovering anything untoward.

Virgilio was sounding subdued. 'He'll live, thank God. He has a compound fracture of his left arm, four broken ribs, a fractured right calf, and concussion. The medics say he's seriously banged up, but they don't think he's sustained any serious internal injuries and he's lucky to be alive. They're keeping him in for the foreseeable future and if all goes well, he should make a full recovery. I haven't been able to see him because he's heavily sedated. They say I'm going to have to wait until the morning to speak to him.' I heard him give a little snort of frustration. 'I can't stop thinking about who might have done it and why.'

He went on to tell me where the accident had happened – right outside Marco's home in the north of the city, ironically not far from the main hospital.

'The impact threw him onto the pavement against a rubbish bin, sending it flying. He was found by a neighbour who heard the noise of the impact but by the time she got outside to see what had happened, the vehicle was long gone. There were no other witnesses and we have no CCTV images yet, but officers are checking shops and houses in the area for any recordings from security cameras, and an appeal has gone out to drivers who were in the area at the time who might have dashcam footage. Hopefully, Marco himself will be able to shed some light on the vehicle involved, but we can't count on it. As you and I both know only too well, victims very often remember little or nothing after catastrophic events like this.'

I checked with Virgilio to see what he intended to do next. 'Is there any way of finding out where Grande, Verdi and Faldo were at the time of the accident? And maybe somebody could take a surreptitious look at their cars for any damage.' Something else occurred to me. 'It may be a genuine accident, but in case it was an attempt to silence him, might it be worth putting an officer outside his door at the hospital for now to prevent the would-be murderer from trying again?'

'My thoughts entirely. I've already arranged a twenty-four-hour guard and as far as checking up on our suspects and their vehicles is concerned, I'll have to do that myself.' There was real frustration and anger in Virgilio's voice. 'I can hardly believe that I can't even trust my own colleagues!'

'Well, you be careful. I don't want to hear any reports of accidents happening to you. Is there anything I can do to help?'

'Thanks for the offer, but I can't think of anything for now. There's no point you even going in to see Marco as you wouldn't be allowed to speak to him. One thing, though: in his absence, I'm taking over the Berg case, and guess who's going to take Marco's place for now? Inspector Roberto Faldo, and he's been parachuted in by Superintendent Vincenzo Grande with the blessing of the *vice questore*. What's that old saying about keeping your friends close but your enemies closer?'

As I digested the ramifications of this, an idea struck me. 'If it's all right with you, why don't you ask me along to help translate next time you visit Berg's villa? I'd be interested to see Faldo close up. Who knows, maybe Superintendent Grande will put in an appearance as well so I could check out both of them at the same time. Would that be okay?'

'Definitely. That looks like being around ten tomorrow. The technician from Switzerland is flying in from Zurich on the early-morning flight. I'll make sure he's met at the airport and taken straight to the villa. As soon as I have final times tomorrow, I'll give you a call. Thanks again, Dan.'

Immediately after he'd rung off, my phone started ringing again. It was the mayor returning my call. When I'd tried to contact him earlier to give him the news of his daughter's boyfriend, he had been in a meeting.

'Good evening, Dan. Sorry it's taken me so long to get back to you. Any news?'

'Yes, indeed, and I think you're going to find that it's good news.'

'That's excellent. Where are you? I'm just about to go home. Do you feel like a drink? I could use one.'

It turned out that he was barely ten minutes away, on the point of leaving his office in the Palazzo Vecchio, the town hall, so we arranged to meet at a café in a little piazza close by. I took Oscar with me and hurried through the crowds to Piazza del Duomo, past the magnificent cathedral, baptistery and belltower and on to the little square. I spotted the mayor already sitting at a table outside on the pavement and went across to him. Although it was early evening, the April air was still pleasantly warm.

When he saw me, he waved. 'Good evening, Dan. I've ordered

two beers, but don't worry if you fancy something else; I'll happily drink both. It's been a busy day.'

I assured him that a cold beer sounded ideal and while Oscar wandered over to make the mayor's acquaintance, I sat down alongside him, looking out into the little piazza only a stone's throw from the Uffizi gallery. This area was bustling with locals going home at the end of the working day and tourists shuttling between the Palazzo Vecchio and Palazzo Pitti. It was already remarkably busy considering that this was still low season. By the time July and August arrived, this whole area would be absolutely heaving with humanity. Little wonder many locals preferred to move out of the city when the summer came, in order to find a bit of peace and quiet – as well as some respite from the cloying heat.

A waiter appeared with two beers, and the mayor and I clinked our glasses together.

I told him what I'd learnt at the theatre this afternoon, finishing with, 'Tiberio seems like an excellent choice as Monica's boyfriend. I can't understand why she wouldn't want you to know about him.'

His reply was interesting. 'Thank you for that, Dan. That's a great relief. For some reason, I had convinced myself that he was a drug dealer or some such. As for why she wouldn't introduce him to us, I'm at a loss to find an explanation. Did you get his surname?'

'I'm afraid not, I didn't want to appear too pushy this afternoon so I didn't ask, but I can easily find that out through the theatre or the university. There can't be many final-year medical students called Tiberio, after all – in fact, I'd be prepared to bet that he's the only one in the whole university. Leave it to me and I'll get the surname tomorrow. As soon as I get it, I'll text it to you.'

He thanked me again and we sat back and relaxed. I could see

that Ugo had been reassured by my news and I could fully understand how he was feeling. No doubt he and his wife had been
imagining all sorts of undesirable characters being involved with
their daughter, and this news must have come as welcome relief.
We chatted about trivia for a few minutes before he asked me
something that stopped me in my tracks.

'Dan, what's your opinion of the police here in Florence?'

'The city police or the national police?' Italy has something
like seven or eight different 'police' forces who theoretically work
together, but between whom rivalries can arise.

'National police, the ones who investigate serious crimes and
arrest robbers and killers.'

'I sometimes work with officers in the murder squad when
English speakers are involved and I've been impressed by their
professionalism. Why, are you having doubts about their ability?'

He turned towards me and lowered his voice, although with
the background noise of the passing pedestrians, we were
unlikely to be overheard. 'Not me personally. I don't know
enough about them to comment, but it was something I heard.'

'Something negative?'

'I know I can trust you to keep this to yourself, Dan, but it was
something the *questore* said to me the other day. He told me he's
worried that he may have a rotten apple on the force. That's the
expression he used: "a rotten apple". I asked him what he meant
by it, and he either couldn't or wouldn't tell me very much. I got
the impression he's concerned that one of his officers might be
involved in some sort of criminal activity.' In response to my
raised eyebrows, he shook his head. 'He didn't say what sort of
criminal activity. In your experience back in London, did you ever
come across that sort of thing?'

I told him about the protection racket I'd been involved in
dismantling and reassured him that the vast majority of police

officers both in Britain and in Italy were on the level. I decided to make no mention of the fact that I was helping Virgilio and Marco sniff out the Florence force's very own 'rotten apple' until I could speak to them. From Virgilio's point of view, I felt sure this would come as very good news and, if I were in his shoes, I would go straight to the *questore*. I gave it a minute or two so as not to look too interested before asking if the *questore* had launched an investigation, and the mayor shrugged.

'I would imagine so, but he didn't give me any detail. It leaves an unpleasant taste in the mouth to think that one of the people who are supposed to be upholding law and order could actually be the one who's breaking it. I hope they catch him... or her.'

This was fascinating. If the *questore* had noticed the irregularities that Virgilio had spotted, maybe there were other officers who had been having doubts about one of their colleagues. Maybe Virgilio, instead of being a lone voice crying in the wilderness, was part of a larger group of honest cops.

Returning to the subject of the mayor's daughter, I mentioned the forthcoming performance of Zebra's *Ultimatum* and asked if he intended going to see it. When he confirmed that he would be there, I suggested that it might be a good opportunity for him and his wife to check out their daughter's beloved for themselves. He received the suggestion with enthusiasm and when he stood up and shook my hand, he was looking a happy man.

I waited until he'd walked away before pulling out my phone and calling Virgilio. I related what the mayor had said and I thought I heard a sigh of relief at the other end.

'That's excellent, Dan. I'm in my office now so I'll see if the *questore*'s in the building and I'll ask if I can talk to him straight away.' I heard him produce what could have been a little chuckle. 'Well, that's one suspect we can remove from the list – although, to be fair, I didn't seriously consider that he might be our villain.

Thanks a lot for passing that on. One interesting piece of news: I ordered a check of Marco's phone records this afternoon and it appears he received a call from a local landline only minutes before he was hit. The call lasted just thirty-seven seconds and when we did a trace, we found that it came from a phone box on the corner of Marco's road and Via Giuliani, barely a couple of hundred metres from his house. That would seem to prove that the "accident" was anything but. I reckon somebody called him and told him there was a family emergency or he was needed back at the station, knowing that this would make him come out of his house and cross the road. And then... smack, he was mowed down.'

'You could well be right – cynical and professional – and if that was the case, the call must have been made by somebody who knew him well, and I wouldn't mind betting it was a member of the force who'd realised that Marco was on their trail. You realise, of course, that this quite possibly means that the would-be killer is also aware that you're involved in the investigation. You'd better watch your back. Have you been able to trace the movements of our main suspects this afternoon?'

'Yes, but it doesn't help very much. All three officers were out and about, away from the station and unaccounted for, at the time of the accident – and the more I think about it, the more I'm convinced that it was no accident. I went down to the parking lot to check the cars, but only Faldo's very smart BMW was there and, no, there were no signs of it having hit anybody. Grande and Verdi were both out in their own vehicles and they won't be back in until tomorrow. I'll take a look as soon as they arrive, but the fact is that any of the three had the opportunity to do it.' He gave a frustrated snort. 'Poor Marco. I feel it was my fault this happened. I shouldn't have got him involved.'

'Don't beat yourself up, Virgilio – apart from anything else, I seem to remember that I was the one who advised you to let him in, so it's as much my fault as yours, but I still think you did the right thing. Marco's a big boy. He knew the risks. That's why he went home to work on the computer. The way I see it, he must have known the person who called him, because he left home straight away. I wonder what emergency the perpetrator dreamt up.' I tried to sound as encouraging as possible. 'When you see him tomorrow morning, he might be able to tell you who made the call, and we can put two and two together.'

'One thing's for sure: I'm going to double the guard outside his hospital room overnight. Here's hoping when he wakes up that he can remember.'

Virgilio didn't sound too confident but then, neither was I.

14

WEDNESDAY MORNING

I got a call from Virgilio at eight-thirty, but it wasn't to announce the arrival of the technician from the safe company or with news that Marco had woken up and started talking.

'There's been another murder.' His tone was grim.

I found myself praying that it wasn't Marco. Surely, the killer hadn't been able to get past the officers on guard. Virgilio's answer came as a relief, but also a surprise.

'Axel Jacobs, age seventy-six, Dutch citizen, found dead in his room at the Grand Hotel.'

This came as a shock – but, given what had happened to David Berg, maybe not such a shock after all. My mind was racing. Why would anybody have wanted to murder Jacobs? This was surely too much of a coincidence. Had Berg and Jacobs been involved in something particularly shady? Jacobs had already told me that their deal had been clandestine, but had it maybe been more than an illicit transaction between two old acquaintances? Had a third party been involved in the deal or even cheated by the two old men? Had the same person who had killed Berg also murdered his associate?

'What was the cause of death?'

'Strangulation. There were bruises to the victim's face so he must have tried to put up a fight, even though he looked frail.'

'Any fingerprints or DNA left behind?'

'Not a thing. A clean, professional hit.'

This sounded ominously similar to Berg's killing. 'Time of death?'

'Gianni says probably between ten and midnight, but he'll know more after the autopsy. The way I see it, Jacobs was in his room late last night when somebody came to his door. He was either expecting the person or the visitor barged his way in. Once inside, the killer strangled Jacobs, who struggled to defend himself, but in vain.'

'Any CCTV footage?'

'We're waiting for it to be passed to us now. The good news is that there are cameras on every floor so, with luck, we should be able to identify the killer.'

'Anything taken from the room?'

'It's been thoroughly ransacked. The killer was definitely looking for something, but whether he found it or not, who knows?'

'I suppose the obvious thing the killer might have been looking for is the cigar box with three hundred thousand euros' worth of gold or jewels in it. The question is, of course, how he knew about what was supposedly a very secret transaction between the two Dutchmen.' I felt I had to state the obvious. 'Do we think it's the same perpetrator who murdered Berg?'

'I'd be surprised if it isn't. Forensics are going through the room as we speak. Let's hope they find something, but if it is Berg's killer, he's unlikely to have been sloppy enough to leave a trace. That guy was a pro and this looks very much the same.' Virgilio's voice was gloomy.

'Is there anything I can do? After all, I'm probably one of the few people Jacobs spoke to while he was here in Florence.'

'It'll be a good idea to give you a formal interview later on, but there's no rush for now. You've already told us the substance of your talk to Jacobs, and Marco's put it on file. I've put Inspector Faldo on the case. He's busy interviewing the staff and guests in the hope that somebody remembers something.'

From his tone, I could tell he wasn't optimistic and neither was I. If the killer had been a pro, there was every chance he would have been able to slip in and out undetected. Even so, I offered a bit of encouragement. 'At least this means you know where Faldo is going to be.'

'Yes, indeed. I'll catch up with him later on after we've had a chance to take a look inside Berg's safe. The flight from Switzerland arrives at nine-fifteen and I really want to go and see Marco first. The hospital tells me that he had a good night and he's awake, so I'm hoping he might be able to tell us more about what happened yesterday. If you're still happy to come along to the villa, let's meet there at ten and hope that we find something of interest in the safe. If there's a hold-up, I'll call you. See you later.'

Because of the continuing warm weather, Anna and I had decided to stay out at my house in the country for a few more days, so it was barely a ten-minute drive to Berg's villa in Signa, and it was with a feeling of considerable anticipation that I arrived there at ten o'clock. Virgilio's car was already there alongside a blue and white squad car and I could see him talking to a uniformed officer. As soon as he saw me, he came across to talk. I had brought Oscar with me and he was so pleased to see Virgilio again, he stood up on his hind legs to be petted.

'*Ciao*, Oscar. *Ciao*, Dan. First, the bad news: Marco can't remember anything about yesterday afternoon at all, apart from going home to work on the computer. He can't remember getting a phone call and he can't recall anything of the accident. The doctor I spoke to told me his memory may return in the course of the next few days, but there's no guarantee. The good news is that he's recovering well and should regain full use of his limbs within a couple of months at most. For what it's worth, I'm going to spread the word that he doesn't remember a thing and that he never will. Hopefully, that'll put off the would-be killer from having another try. I'm also keeping the officers outside Marco's door until he's well enough to leave hospital.'

'Good idea. It's better to be safe than sorry.' I nodded slowly. 'What about the cars belonging to Verdi and Grande? Any signs of damage?'

'Nothing at all, I'm afraid.'

I lowered my voice. 'Did you manage to speak to the *questore* yesterday?'

'He was at a conference in Venice and he'll be back around lunchtime today. I've left word with his secretary for him to contact me as soon as he returns – as a matter of urgency.'

'And the technician from the Swiss safe company?'

'His flight was on time and he's inside the villa at the moment, fiddling with the assortment of gizmos he's brought with him. He's confident he can get it open this morning, but he wasn't prepared to hazard a guess as to how long it'll take.' He gestured back in the direction of the villa. 'I thought in the meantime, it might be useful for me to speak to the members of the family. You've met them already, of course, but I'd quite like to get a look at them before we get sight of the will. Feel like coming with me?'

We went over to the front door and rang the bell. Ines, the housekeeper, greeted us and showed us into the lounge where the family were once again sitting on the two sofas in exactly the same positions as before. At first sight, it looked almost as if they hadn't stirred for three days. I introduced Virgilio and translated for him when necessary, although his English was well up to the task. Casper Berg was quick to ask if there had been any developments. Virgilio answered with a question.

'Does the name Axel Jacobs mean anything to you?'

All three siblings nodded and Emma spoke for them all. 'He's a well-known trader in jewels and precious metals. He used to be based in Amsterdam like we are, but he's now moved to Antwerp. We occasionally buy gemstones from him.'

Casper went on to clarify. 'Most of our business these days is buying and selling finished jewellery. Back in our father's day, the company also did a lot of diamond cutting, manufacture of rings, bracelets and necklaces, often using gold and precious stones purchased from Jacobs. He knows our father, but he's never spoken about him with us.'

Emma added dryly, 'Mainly because he knew we didn't want to speak about our father to anyone. Why do you ask? Is Mr Jacobs involved in some way?'

'I'm afraid he was found dead in his hotel room here this morning.'

Casper looked genuinely shocked. 'You mean he was here in Florence? Do you think his death was suspicious?'

Virgilio nodded. 'I'm afraid he's been murdered. There's no doubt about it. Can you think of any reason why anybody might have wanted him dead?'

They all shook their heads and, as they did so, I studied their faces without seeing any immediate signs of guilt.

Virgilio then moved on. 'As you may have seen, the technician from the safe company has arrived, so we should gain access to your father's safe later this morning. We understand that your father and Mr Jacobs had some kind of deal going on involving a considerable value of gold or precious stones. Now that Jacobs has been killed, we're afraid that there may be a connection between the two deaths, and we would advise you to be very cautious if you go out anywhere.'

Emma looked appalled. 'You think we might be in danger?'

'It seems likely that the two deaths are connected in some way, so it's a sensible precaution for you to take care when you're out and about. You're most probably in no danger at all, but I felt I needed to warn you to be careful. Stick together as far as possible and avoid wandering around lonely places, especially in the dark. Have you been visiting Florence while you've been waiting around?'

Casper nodded. 'Yes, on and off. It's a beautiful city and none of us have been here before.'

I asked a question of my own. 'As the *commissario* says, it's probably best if you stick together. Do you usually go around as a group or individually?'

Casper answered. 'A bit of both. Helga and I and Emma and Guido mostly go around together while Luuc prefers to be on his own.'

Luuc spoke up. 'I find I can see so much more if I'm on my own.' The suspicion dawned on me that maybe the others preferred it that way. Was Luuc a bit of a loner and, if so, did that make him suspicious?

I tried to keep my tone as friendly as possible. 'Well, just be careful. What about food? Have you been dining out? I must say, since coming to live here, I've fallen in love with Tuscan food.'

They all nodded and a brief conversation ensued during which it was clear that they had been out most evenings, including last night. Although the two couples spontaneously and conveniently provided alibis for each other, Luuc told us he'd been on his own and so had no alibi for last night around the time that Jacobs had been murdered. Whether this was significant or not would no doubt emerge in due course, but there was something about him that didn't sit well with me.

Virgilio asked them when they had arrived in Florence and it turned out that the two couples had travelled here on Friday and had stayed in a hotel on the night when their father had been murdered, while Luuc claimed to have set off later, arriving before lunch on Saturday. I met Virgilio's eye for a moment. On this basis, it was clear that, travelling alone, Luuc Berg might even have set off earlier and got here in time to murder his father and dispose of the body before meeting his siblings the next day. The big question was why – just hatred of the man who had destroyed their happy family or something else?

Virgilio told them that he would inform them when the safe had been opened and he had had a chance to look at the contents. At that point, he would relay his findings to the family. There was an air of anticipation in the room. It looked as though their father's will would finally be read.

We left them there and went up to the old man's study where we found a uniformed officer standing guard while the Swiss specialist was hard at work with a stethoscope and a strange electrical contraption clamped onto the door of the safe making a humming/clicking sound. The technician looked around as we came in. He was probably around my age with a receding hairline and one of those funny little beards that just circled the jaw, without a moustache. He greeted Virgilio.

'*Commissario*, perfect timing.' He spoke Italian with a strong Germanic accent. He glanced down at the mystery machine attached to the safe door. 'It's just past ten-nineteen. In exactly forty-two seconds, the safe should be open.'

Virgilio handed me a pair of disposable gloves and produced a satisfied smile. 'Not long now. Thirty seconds and counting.'

And then we might finally learn more about why David Berg
and Axel Jacobs had been murdered.

15

WEDNESDAY MORNING

The man from Switzerland was true to his word. At exactly ten twenty, there was a final beep from the machine followed by a solid clunk. The technician spun the handle and the safe door swung open. The door and walls were about four inches thick and I could see how difficult it would have been for a thief to get in without destroying the contents – and probably half the villa as well. This had been built to withstand most things. Virgilio and I stood there and studied the contents closely while the technician set about packing his tools away as if safe cracking were the most normal occupation in the world. I wondered idly how much he would be able to make if he ever decided to embrace the dark side.

There were three shelves inside the safe and just about the first thing I spotted on the top shelf was a yellow and brown cigar box, roughly the size of a big book. Alongside it was a little pile of five shiny gold bars, each roughly the size of a pack of cards. Next to these were a number of jewellery boxes and clear plastic bags containing different-coloured precious stones. The middle shelf held a pile of documents, while on the bottom shelf, there were three large gold ingots, each almost the size of a packet of biscuits. I wondered how much these might be worth – certainly these alone fully justified the installation of such a secure safe. Virgilio reached in and picked up a handful of the documents. On top of them all was a long envelope and I heard him give a grunt of satisfaction. He held it up and I could see that it had *Casper* handwritten on it.

'This looks like David Berg's will.' He set it down on top of the safe and started flicking through the other documents.

I grabbed the rest of the pile in my gloved hands and started to go through them. It didn't take long to realise that they were mostly certificates of authentication, in particular, certificates attesting to the place of origin of each of the jewels and precious metals in the safe. My eye happened on a certificate headed *Emirates Gold*, confirming the authenticity of a 99.9 per cent pure gold bullion bar with a weight of 400 troy ounces. I had no idea what this meant in real terms so I squatted down and lifted one of the gold bars on the bottom shelf – and it wasn't easy. I pulled it out and weighed it in my hand, reckoning that it had to be at least ten kilos. That meant that this relatively small piece of metal weighed the same as half a dozen full bottles of wine, if not more. This meant that these three bars amounted to at least thirty kilos of pure gold. These plus the smaller gold bars and the gemstones were the proof that Berg had been a very, very wealthy man. I replaced the gold bar and glanced at the envelope marked *Casper* on top of the safe. Who was going to inherit the gold and all the other stuff belonging to David Berg?

I returned the pile of papers to the middle shelf and glanced across at Virgilio. 'All right with you if I take a look inside Jacobs's cigar box? I'm dying to see what's in it.'

'Go for it. I'm keen to see for myself.'

I picked up the cigar box and brought it out. It was double the size of the big gold ingots – almost as big as the T-bone steak we had eaten at the weekend – but it weighed far less than the ingots. I set it down on the desk and opened the lid, noting the wording *Montecristo No. 4* on the top as I did so. Inside, there was a layer of cotton wool and when I delicately pulled this out of the way, I was almost dazzled by the blaze of reflected light that emanated from the box. There, in front of me, was a jumbled mass of diamonds in all shapes and sizes ranging from one as big as a broad bean to others little bigger than grains of rice. There must have been several hundred diamonds in there. Some were lighter, some darker, some so rough, they looked little more than random seaside pebbles, but most were crystal clear – literally. I was impressed to hear even the hitherto reserved Swiss technician gasp in amazement, and the uniformed officer at the door took a step nearer to admire the contents of the box. Only Oscar, happily snoozing by the window, failed to be impressed. Now, if it had been a T-bone steak...

'So that's what three hundred thousand euros looks like.' There was awe in Virgilio's voice. He picked up his phone and called the *questura*, asking for Forensics to send a team as soon as possible. Putting his phone down again, he looked up. 'I want fingerprints from everything, particularly the cigar box. If we find prints belonging to Jacobs, that might help his case in establishing his ownership of the diamonds – not that it'll do him much good now, poor man.'

'Then what happens to this stuff? Do you take it away? Does it go into a bank vault?' I glanced at the Swiss technician. 'What if we left it here? Can you give us the combination or can we set a new one?'

'When I opened the safe, all settings automatically returned to default factory settings. That means that the combination is ABCD12345. It's easy to set a new combination with the door open, using a combination of nine letters or numbers. I would suggest that if you change the combination, the contents of the safe will probably be more secure left where they are. This is one of our top-of-the-range models and I doubt if there's anybody else in Europe who could open it.' His tone wasn't boastful; he was just stating a fact.

Virgilio nodded. 'That sounds like an excellent idea. I very much doubt if the *questore* would have wanted the responsibility of transporting and looking after hundreds of thousands of euros' worth of jewels and gold.'

A thought occurred to me. 'What about the family? Are you planning on letting them take a look?'

Virgilio shook his head decisively. 'No, I don't want any more people than necessary poking around in here. We have to talk to them about their father's will and we can give them a rough idea of what's in the safe at that stage. How heavy do you reckon those big gold bars are?'

'At least ten kilos. They weigh much more than you'd think.'

The Swiss technician cleared his throat. 'If you don't mind my butting in, gentlemen, I think you'll find those are standard bullion bars, 400 troy ounces each, and they weigh just under twelve and a half kilos each.' He paused to do some rapid mental arithmetic. 'Three of those at today's gold price add up to roughly two and a half million euros, Swiss francs or US dollars. The smaller one-kilo bars on the top shelf are worth about sixty thousand euros each.'

Virgilio and I exchanged looks. On that basis, the five smaller gold bars added up to three hundred thousand euros, presumably the payment that Jacobs had handed over in exchange for the diamonds in the box. Virgilio whistled in amazement. 'So with Jacobs's diamonds, plus the extra three hundred thousand in gold, plus however much all these other gemstones are worth, that makes a total of well over three million euros sitting here.' Virgilio turned to the technician. 'I'd be grateful if you'd show me how to set the new combination now. The sooner we get this door locked again, the happier I'll be.' He switched his attention to the young constable. 'And Linetti, I want you to keep your lips firmly sealed about what you've just seen. Am I clear? Not even to your mother. The last thing we need is for a bunch of local villains to descend on this place looking for treasure.'

After the safe door had once again been locked, Virgilio picked up the envelope presumably containing David Berg's will and turned to me. 'Shall we take Oscar for a little walk in the garden?'

The magic word immediately had Oscar on his feet and heading for the door. Virgilio shook hands with the technician and thanked him, leaving Constable Linetti to drive him back to the airport as soon as the Swiss had finished collecting all his bits and pieces. Virgilio and I followed Oscar down the stairs and let ourselves out of the front door. David Berg's garden was a large one, divided into different levels supported by dry stone walls, and we followed a path that wound its way up through the olive trees and aromatic rosemary shrubs. Once we were suitably far from curious ears, we sat down on one of the walls and Virgilio turned to me. The Swiss technician wasn't the only one to have been doing some mental arithmetic.

'At a rough guess, I reckon this house has to be worth at least two or three million euros, probably more. In the safe, there's at least that amount or more, plus there's the shop on the Ponte Vecchio and its contents. David Berg was a very wealthy man.' He held up the envelope. 'Let's see who gets all his money.'

He slit the end of the envelope with a penknife, slid out the contents and confirmed to me that this was indeed the old man's will, accompanied by a covering letter. The will was written in

Italian and Virgilio read it out loud. It contained few surprises. There was a sum of ten thousand euros to be paid to Signora Ines Bianchi for her years as what Berg described as 'a faithful servant', and the rest of his considerable fortune was to be divided equally between his three children. When he had finished reading, Virgilio caught my eye.

'With the villa, that means around two million euros each, even without Axel Jacobs's cigar box. For most people, that could be ample grounds to consider committing murder, but maybe not in this case. Marco was in touch with the Dutch police on Monday, and I got a communication from them this morning indicating that the three shops in Amsterdam are doing well, and Berg's children are already rich in their own right. On that basis, I fail to see what advantage there might have been in it for any of them to murder the old man, especially as the money was coming to them before long anyway. What do you think, Dan?'

'I agree, although they didn't know for sure the provisions of the old man's will. But maybe money wasn't the motive. Maybe Berg was killed for another reason, something that links him to the second victim.' I thought it worth suggesting the other hypothesis. 'And of course, it's possible we're looking for two different killers and the two murders aren't related.'

Virgilio nodded. 'Yes, I'm struggling to see how the two murders can be linked, although the fact that both men were Dutch and both in the jewellery trade makes it so much more likely. With such a large amount of money at stake, surely the motive for both murders has to be robbery. Maybe the killer knew that Jacobs had come to Florence to buy the diamonds from Berg. It's possible that the murder at the Ponte Vecchio was the killer looking for the diamonds there and, when he drew a blank, he then tracked Jacobs down and killed him when it was clear he didn't have either the diamonds or the payment for them.'

'Whatever the motive, I find it suspicious that Luuc Berg has no alibi for the times of either of the two murders. And don't let's forget that he's in the jewellery trade as well, so he might have been following Jacobs all the way from the Netherlands.'

Virgilio nodded. 'You could be right, and it was a family affair. How about this? Maybe David Berg was killed by his son in revenge for going off and leaving the family. Before you say it, the problem with that scenario is why did it take his son thirty years to get round to doing it? I might have the answer to that. They said their mother died only four months ago. What if the mother's death tipped Luuc over the edge, and he came here looking for revenge?'

I could see the logic behind this theory, but I wasn't convinced. 'When Luuc told us that they'd loved their mother, I could feel a lot of emotion in his voice, but I'm not sure I see him as a murderer. From what you've been hearing, he wasn't short of money either, so the idea of him killing his father and then Jacobs for the diamonds seems unlikely, but the fact remains, however, that he doesn't have an alibi for either night. What does the covering letter say?'

Virgilio looked at it briefly before shrugging his shoulders and passing it across to me. 'How's your Dutch?'

In fact, with the aid of my very rusty German and my phone, it was relatively easy to get the gist of the letter and for the first time, I sensed some genuine emotion from David Berg. The letter was, in effect, an apology to his children for abandoning them and their mother. He explained quite touchingly how he had fallen in love with Claudia Greco – describing her as the love of his life – and when she had chosen to return to Italy, he had had no option but to follow her. He told the children how much he had missed them and how he hoped that the provisions of his will would at least make them think slightly better of him. He even signed it *'veel liefs'*, which I took to be 'lots of love'.

I gave Virgilio a rough translation before handing the letter back to him. He took it from me, folded it together with the will and slipped the two sheets back into the envelope. He stood up and glanced in the direction of the villa. 'Now I think it's time to pass this on to Casper and the others. I want to see their reactions.'

'It'll be very interesting to see the looks on their faces when you tell them there's over three million euros in the safe upstairs.'

The reactions of the three siblings to the provisions of the will were mixed. Casper looked surprised and pleased, his sister looked equally surprised, but studiously avoided showing any signs of pleasure. Luuc, on the other hand, just nodded a couple of times and demonstrated virtually no emotion whatsoever. The covering letter drew an expression of satisfaction from Casper, real tears from his sister and, again, absolutely no reaction whatsoever from Luuc.

When Virgilio informed them of the contents of the safe and the approximate value of what was in there, Casper and Emma looked pleased, while Luuc still remained expressionless. Virgilio asked them if they could delay leaving Florence for another twenty-four hours, ostensibly so that Forensics could study the contents of the safe before handing everything over to the family. While this was no doubt true, I felt pretty sure that this would also be so that Virgil could question them individually – particularly Luuc – before they disappeared back to the Netherlands.

I took a final look at their faces before we left the room. Was one of them a murderer, maybe even a multiple murderer? By the sound of it, we had only twenty-four hours to find out.

16

WEDNESDAY LUNCHTIME

I left Virgilio at the villa, standing guard as Forensics sifted through the contents of the safe. When I got back to the office, I found that Zebra had called and left a message for me with Lina. It didn't go into any detail but just indicated that she needed to see me as a matter of urgency. She had left a phone number so I sat down and called her back, but without getting a response. I decided to try her later and settled down to answer the emails received since yesterday. It looked as though the next few weeks were going to be busy as one of the emails was from a large company, asking me to investigate possible industrial espionage, and another was from a woman whose ex-husband was stalking her.

I had just finished composing detailed proposals for both potential clients and I was starting to think about lunch when my phone rang. It was Virgilio.

'*Ciao*, Dan, are you free for lunch?'

'Yes, I was just thinking about getting something to eat. Where do you fancy?'

'Out of town. I'll come and pick you up if you like.' He lowered his voice. 'I've had a hurried conversation with the *questore* and he'd like to take both of us out for lunch to a place he knows where we can talk freely.'

'I wonder why he wants me to tag along. He's never met me.' In fact, I had a good idea of the *questore's* reasons, and Virgilio confirmed my supposition.

'Because he trusts you. He knows how helpful you've been to us on a number of occasions. You're outside the force and, the way things are at the moment, almost everybody in the force is suspect.' He sounded understandably frustrated.

A practical consideration occurred to me. 'I've got Oscar with me. I can probably ask Lina to watch him for me if necessary.'

'That's all right, I've already mentioned Oscar, and the *questore* knows you and he are a double act. The place we're meeting has a secluded terrace where we'll be able to talk without being overheard and Oscar can join us. Have you ever been to Colonnata? The restaurant's a short way up the hill from there.'

I had vaguely heard of the village in the hills to the north of Florence but I hadn't been there, or to the *questore's* chosen restaurant, before. Virgilio came and collected me and we cut through the lunchtime traffic easily with the aid of his flashing blue lights. We went out through the suburbs until we reached open countryside and started to climb. Barely five or six kilometres after Colonnata, we came upon the Montagna Nera restaurant. This had been created inside an old farmhouse on the flank of one of the first foothills of the Apennines, a thousand feet above Florence and the valley of the River Arno. It was a charming old stone building with dusty green shutters on the windows and an enormous wisteria running almost the entire length of the building. I could well imagine how impressive this would look when it bloomed in a few months' time.

The *questore*, Massimo Livornese, was an unexpectedly small man. He was probably only in his mid-sixties but he had wisps of snow-white hair on his head that made him look older. He did not, however, look senile. He was sitting outside at an isolated table at the far end of a panoramic terrace overlooking Florence and he stood up remarkably nimbly to shake hands with us when he saw us. He patted Oscar's head and handed him a couple of breadsticks from the table. Clearly, this was a man who knew the way to my dog's heart.

'Commissario Pisano, good afternoon. Signor Armstrong, thank you so much for coming. Thank you also for the help you've given so generously to the force over the past year or two. I appreciate it immensely. Sit down, please, and let's order some food. Although it may seem a bit strange up here in the hills, the chef specialises in fish and seafood and I can thoroughly recommend his mixed seafood grill. Alternatively, they also do some excellent grilled meat if you prefer that.'

I had eaten more than enough grilled meat over the past few days, so I opted for the grilled fish willingly and the others followed suit. The *questore* insisted that we try the chef's special *pappardelle ai frutti di mare* first and I braced myself for yet another mammoth meal. This evening's walk with Oscar was going to have to be a long one to compensate – either that or I was going to have to consider getting myself a whole new wardrobe.

Once the order had been placed, and the waiter had brought us a bottle of cold white wine and a bottle of mineral water, the *questore* turned to the matter at hand and addressed me directly.

'Signor Armstrong, Commissario Pisano has no doubt told you about the problem facing us, and I'm most grateful to you for sparing the time to assist us. Are you fully aware of what we're dealing with?'

'As I understand it, sir, somebody in the Florence police force has been tampering with the files, in particular those relating to the deaths of two *extracomunitari* at Santa Maria Novella station. From what Commissario Pisano has told me, only an officer at inspector level or above would be able to make such changes to your records so it narrows down the list of suspects considerably.'

He nodded approvingly. 'Precisely. And now we have a situation where one of our officers has been seriously injured in an apparent hit-and-run accident, and, from what Commissario Pisano tells me, the accident may well have been a deliberate attempt by a traitor within our ranks to kill Inspector Innocenti.' There was horror and anger in his tone. 'We must catch this swine before he can do any more damage.'

Virgilio ran through the facts before us – which were all too few – and the *questore* listened in silence, occasionally nodding his head. He didn't take notes and neither did we. This was highly confidential stuff and best not committed to paper. The trouble was, of course, that we didn't have very much to go on. Even the identities of the two asylum seekers murdered at the station were unknown. For all we knew, there might even have been others whose files had been removed. Both victims had been poorly dressed, without any personal belongings, and it was hard to see what possible reason there might have been for their murders, and even less for why a senior officer in the Florence force should have risked his career to conceal what had happened. I raised the possibility that it might have been some sort of vigilante, as previously suggested by Marco, and Livornese nodded.

'It's no secret that there are officers in our force and other forces whose views are to the right of centre, in some cases far to the right of centre. I suppose it's possible that there might be somebody here who has decided that the only way to deal with immigrants is to kill them. The problem is going to be rooting this person out.'

Virgilio answered. 'That's what Marco Innocenti was doing yesterday afternoon, sir: checking the social media of our prime suspects to see if any of them had expressed extreme political views. I found nothing and, from what he could remember when I spoke to him this morning, he also drew a blank – but his memory is still very shaky. As I mentioned to you earlier back in your office, my gut feeling is that there are three senior officers particularly worthy of consideration, but of course it could well be somebody completely different.' His tone conveyed the frustration he was feeling.

I added a few words of my own. 'I also did a sweep of social media and other mentions on the Internet of these three officers but without finding anything sinister. Yes, there's the possibility that one or more of them might be living beyond their means or might have some questionable habits when it comes to women, but I certainly didn't find a smoking gun by any means.'

Our conversation was interrupted by the arrival of the pasta course. A waiter appeared bearing a large platter heaped with broad strips of pappardelle and covered in a thick, brown sauce peppered with mussels and clams, whose aroma had Oscar on his feet, nose pointed unerringly at the food above him. I handed him down another breadstick and he settled at my feet with a heavy sigh that clearly spoke of his disappointment, but I hardened my heart. I knew by now that if I were to give him all the food he wanted, I wouldn't be the only one with an unwanted spare tyre around my waist.

The food was excellent and, inevitably, conversation stilled for a few minutes while we cleared our plates. Once the waiter had removed the empty dishes, Questore Livornese addressed the nub of our problem.

'We now have to decide what, if anything, we can do about this. Commissario Pisano, do you have any suggestions?'

Virgilio pointed across the table at me. 'Signor Armstrong has been kind enough to do a bit of online research, as he says, and he's taken the trouble to check out the homes of the three main suspects. I've also been doing what I can online and at HQ, but, as I have to be very careful not to arouse suspicion, there's a limit to what I've been able to accomplish. All we have for now are suspicions, no proof.'

I told him more about what I'd discovered about the three men and we discussed possible financial problems any of them might have, as well as the likelihood of one or more of them laying themselves open to blackmail because of a penchant for younger women. In particular, when I mentioned that Giuseppe Verdi, the *vice questore*, appeared to have a reputation as a womaniser, I could see that this didn't come as news to his boss.

'Verdi's always been that way inclined, I'm afraid. My wife knows his wife well and it's clear she's reaching the end of her tether with him. But do I see him as a murderer, a multiple murderer? No, I don't.' He stopped and gave a helpless shrug of the shoulders. 'But stranger things have happened.'

As the *questore* finished speaking, Virgilio's phone beeped and he picked it up. He studied the message he'd just received very carefully and then handed it across the table to me. 'I've just been sent this. This individual was caught on CCTV in the Grand Hotel last night. As you can see, there's little doubt he's the person who murdered Jacobs.'

I took the phone eagerly and studied the four photos, all timed at around half past ten the previous night. One had clearly been taken on a landing, one in a corridor and one actually showed the figure entering what was presumably Jacobs's room.

The fourth photo was of the man exiting via the lobby and I was immediately struck by the appearance of the killer. He looked quite tall, almost certainly a man, and he was wearing dark trousers and a dark hoodie, pulled up so as to conceal his head. I passed it across the table to the *questore* and shot a question at Virgilio.

'I haven't seen the CCTV footage of the man who murdered David Berg on the Ponte Vecchio, but, from the description Marco gave me, this looks like the same perpetrator. Have you seen the Berg footage?'

Virgilio nodded. 'I have and it's him, I'm sure of it.' He looked across at his boss. 'I imagine you're familiar with the circumstances of the murders of the two Dutchmen, sir, but to my mind, this unmistakably links them together. Both Signor Armstrong and I felt that it was too much of a coincidence for the two murders not to be connected, but with these photos, we can now be almost certain that they were.'

Livornese studied the photos carefully. 'Very interesting. I hope very much that you catch this man but, above all, I hope you manage to catch the traitor in our midst.'

There was a serious expression on Virgilio's face when he responded. 'You can rely on me, sir. As far as the deaths of the two Dutchmen are concerned, now that we've established what looks like a definite link between Berg and Jacobs, it seems probable that both murders were committed by somebody trying to get hold of Berg's diamonds, Jacobs's three hundred thousand euros in payment, or David Berg's cache of jewellery – or all three. This was either the work of a professional jewel thief or it might be the work of a member of the Berg family. They're all involved with the jewel trade and one of the family, in particular, has no alibi for the times of either murder.'

I nodded in agreement and Virgilio glanced across at me. 'When we get back to Florence, the first thing I'm going to do is to sit down and have a serious talk to Luuc Berg about exactly where he was and what he was doing on those two occasions.' An afterthought came to him. 'And while I'm there, I intend to check the three Dutch-registered cars for signs of damage consistent with what happened to Inspector Innocenti, just in case they tried to eliminate him. Now that we've established a link between the deaths of David Berg and Axel Jacobs, both Dutch jewellers, this brings the family into play once again.'

Further conversation was interrupted by the arrival of a massive wooden board laden with at least half a dozen types of grilled fish and seafood, ranging from tuna steaks and squid rings to prawns on wooden skewers. Another waiter appeared and placed a big bowl of mixed salad alongside the fish and, just in case we were still feeling hungry, a large dish with a mountain of fries on it. I distinctly heard a frustrated grunt from under the table as Oscar did his best to indicate that he was at imminent risk of dying of hunger. I kept my resolve but the *questore* had no such scruples, and, in the course of the next twenty minutes or so, Oscar found himself on the receiving end of several prawns, a couple of squid rings, a succulent piece of tuna and even more breadsticks. Tonight's walk was going to have to be very, very long.

It was an excellent meal, but I was sure we all came away feeling frustrated. Yes, the CCTV evidence from Jacobs's hotel had maybe provided a bit of good news as far as the Berg/Jacobs case was concerned, but the problem of identifying and catching the police officer responsible for deleting the asylum seeker files and maybe murdering the two men at the station remained a real problem, complicated by the fact that everything had to be done in the strictest secrecy. The *questore* promised that he would do his best to keep his eye on Verdi, the *vice questore*, while Virgilio offered to attempt some sort of surveillance of Superintendent Grande. Inspector Faldo was the easiest of the three to keep tabs on now that he'd been brought in to fill Marco's shoes. Whether any of this would result in a breakthrough, however, remained highly questionable.

17

WEDNESDAY AFTERNOON

When Virgilio dropped me back at the office, I tried phoning Zebra again, but without success, so I decided to drive over there to see her. If all went well, while I was there, I would also be able to find out the surname of handsome Tiberio, boyfriend of the mayor's daughter.

When I got to the theatre, there were very few cars or scooters to be seen and I hoped Zebra hadn't gone off somewhere. The front door was locked, but the side door I had urged her to keep locked at all times was predictably open. Oscar had already worked out that he was on the territory of his new best friend and he trotted in, tail wagging. I followed him into the auditorium but found nobody. The stage was also empty except for a load of timber and a carpenter's workbench but, again, there was nobody about. I checked the other rooms one by one until I finally reached the room we had designated as the one where anything valuable had to be kept. It came as no surprise to me to see the door half-open. The surprise was what awaited me inside.

Oscar disappeared into the room and I pushed the door fully open to reveal Zebra sitting by the table with my very happy dog trying to climb onto her lap – but she didn't look anything like as happy as he did. In fact, she was crying, and from her red eyes, it was clear she'd been crying for quite some time. I hurried across to her.

'Zebra, what's the matter? Has something happened? Oscar, leave the lady alone.'

She looked up and wiped the back of her hand across her tear-stained face. Without a word, she pointed to her phone, lying on the table. I went over and tapped the screen to find myself looking at a photo of a man with his hand in the pocket of one of the coats hanging on a row of hooks. I recognised the room as the actors' common room where we'd positioned the spy camera, and there could be no doubt about it: the thief was none other than Paolo with the scruffy overalls, the actor who couldn't be bothered to learn his lines.

I pulled up a chair and sat down alongside her. By this time, Oscar had realised that she was unhappy and had also positioned himself beside her, placing a big, black paw on her lap in a show of canine solidarity. I gave her another minute or so to collect herself before I spoke.

'That's Paolo in the photo, isn't it?' She nodded mutely and I went on. 'Have you spoken to him yet?'

She nodded again, reached for her tissue, and blew her nose before speaking. 'Yes, he came in shortly after I spoke to your secretary on the phone. I was still furious, then I really let rip at him.'

'And what was his reaction?'

'He burst into tears. He cried like a baby and gradually told me all about it. He confessed that he's developed a serious drug habit and it's taking every cent that he has. He told me how terribly sorry he was – and I believed him – but he said he couldn't help himself.' She wiped her eyes again and looked up at me. 'I know a thing or two about drugs and I'm surprised I didn't realise sooner that he had a habit. Of course that's the reason he keeps forgetting his lines. I know how addiction can change a person, but the fact is that I can't keep a thief in the company and I made that clear to him. I gave him the name of somebody who helped me to quit my habit, and I've told him to give her a call. He went off in tears, and I've been crying ever since.'

I tried to be as supportive as possible and to keep it light. 'My grandmother always used to say that the answer to all of life's problems is a good cup of tea. Why don't I go and make you one? In fact, I'll make some for both of us.'

She nodded and even managed to produce a hint of a smile. I left Oscar with her to add his support and by the time I came back with two cups of tea, the tears had stopped, although she was clearly still deeply troubled. I handed her a cup and decided to address the elephant in the room.

'What happens about the play? You'll have to find a last-minute replacement, won't you?'

'We'll have to cancel. There are a couple of girls who could help out, but we need a man and I don't have one. There's no alternative...' Her voice tailed off dejectedly. 'And it was going to be the first ever performance of *Ultimatum*. To make matters worse, this will mean giving back the money we've received for advance tickets and I've already had to spend quite a lot of it.'

'Surely there must be somebody who can step in.'

She shook her head. 'I've been sitting here phoning all the actors I know, but none of them can make it at such short notice...' Her voice tailed off and she suddenly looked up at me. 'Wait a minute, didn't you say you used to do a bit of acting?'

Even Oscar raised his head at that and shot me a curious glance. I was quick to start making my excuses. 'That was forty years ago, Zebra. Besides, all the other actors are half my age.'

'Ah, but I wrote that part, the part of Cesare the mechanic, for a middle-aged man. You'd be perfect for it.' She reached over and clasped my hand in hers. 'You've already helped me so much, Dan, but if you do this for me, I'll love you forever.'

'But it's all in Italian, and I'm English.'

'But you speak such lovely Italian; you'll be fine.'

There's an Italian word for what she was doing – *insaponare*. The literal translation is to soap somebody up, and it means that she was doing her best to charm me into accepting the part by plying me with compliments. I had another couple of attempts at explaining why I was a poor substitute before I realised that she really had a very simple choice. Either she cast an Englishman who hadn't stepped onto a stage for over forty years, or she would have to cancel the whole thing, which, of course, had been her brainchild from its creation to its first ever performance. I finally let her show me what the part entailed and I had to admit that there weren't that many lines for me to learn. Luckily for me, Cesare the mechanic was a man of very few words. Grudgingly, I agreed to take a look at the script tonight and present myself for a run-through with her next morning and a final dress rehearsal on Friday afternoon.

'All right, just to help out, I'll do my best, but if I end up tongue-tied and the whole thing grinds to a halt, you have been warned.'

'You'll manage perfectly, I know you will.' She jumped to her feet and came over to shower me with kisses, leaving my Labrador looking positively jealous. 'I'll call Monica and Tiberio now to tell them it's back on. I was speaking to them just before you arrived and they were understandably bitterly disappointed. They'll be so happy when they hear that Cousin Dan has agreed to help out.'

'I hope they're still happy when they see me on stage. Hopefully, the audience will be blown away by their performances and they won't notice the mistakes that I make.' This reminded me of the other reason why I'd come here this afternoon, so I asked as casually as I could. 'Who are they anyway? Monica and Tiberio who? What're their surnames? I need to know for when they're famous.'

'She's Monica Gallo and he's Tiberio Carbone.' I could see that she was already thinking about everything she would now have to do to revive the play, so I didn't interrupt her. Instead, I just sat there and sipped my tea. The tea had been a random supermarket brand and the only milk in the fridge had been that awful long-life stuff, but it was better than nothing. I wondered idly if Zebra realised that Monica was the mayor's daughter. Gallo is a very common surname in Italy and it was possible that Monica had kept her family background a secret so as not to stick out like a sore thumb in this more plebian environment. Certainly, Zebra had never even hinted at this to me, and when the mayor showed up in the audience on Saturday night, there was likely to be quite a surprise in store for her. I had to wait several minutes before she looked up, that same little smile once more appearing on her face as she picked up her phone. 'Dan, you've saved my life; the show must and will go on. As Julius Caesar said as he crossed the Rubicon, *"Alea iacta est"* – the die is cast.'

I couldn't help pointing out, 'And we all know what happened to Julius Caesar, don't we?'

'It'll be fine, Dan. You'll be fine, I just know it.'

I wished I shared her confidence but, as she had said, the die was cast and I was in it now – up to my neck.

While I finished my tea and tried not to contemplate the terrifying prospect of drying up in front of the whole audience, Zebra phoned Monica Gallo and Tiberio Carbone and, from what I could hear, they were both delighted that the play was back on again. By the time the call ended, a proper smile had returned to Zebra's face and the first thing she did was to stand up, throw her arms around my neck and kiss me some more. She then turned back to Oscar and did the same to him. I was glad she had kissed me before she kissed him. He does tend to stick his nose into some insalubrious places.

'Thank you so much, Dan. You've saved the day. And please don't worry, I'll be close by to prompt you if you forget your lines – but I'm sure you won't need me.' I didn't share her optimism but I decided not to spoil her mood. Her depression had passed and she was looking excited once again. I was happy for her and she was beaming at me. 'Now I need to get hold of Dario and tell him to come back and get the scenery finished.'

I stood up. 'I'm glad to be able to help. All right with you if I collect my camera now? And then I'd better go home and learn my lines.'

I had only just finished removing the spy camera when Amélie the cleaner arrived with a broad smile on her face. I asked how she had heard the news so quickly and she looked puzzled.

'What news?'

I told her that the play had been cancelled but that it was back on again. In response, she clapped her hands together and her smile became even broader. I felt I had to ask if there was another reason why she had come in looking so happy and she came over to me to explain, the excitement in her voice almost palpable. 'We're finally leaving Florence next week and heading to England. I'm so happy, I could sing. Not that Zebra hasn't been a great help, but it's just fantastic to know that we're progressing.'

'So this means you've been able to collect together enough money for the journey?'

'Well, with a little bit of help. My brother-in-law, Vanda's

husband, has arrived and he's brought enough money for us to
continue our journey.'

'He wasn't travelling with you?'

She shook her head. 'No, he's been working in the mines over
in the DRC. He made his way here by a different route.'

'The DRC? Sorry, my geography isn't great.'

'The Democratic Republic of the Congo. A lot of the men in
our country go there to find work. Ours is a very poor nation.'

'And he managed to smuggle cash out of the country? That
sounds risky.'

A sour expression appeared on her face, but only for a few
moments. 'You're right, he didn't bring much cash. The people
smugglers and the gangs would have taken it off him.' She
glanced around and lowered her voice. 'He sewed three little
diamonds into the hem of his trouser leg.'

I tried my best to keep my expression neutral, although my
brain had suddenly erupted into a fury of conjecture. 'Diamonds?
Was he working in a diamond mine?'

'No, a copper mine, but there are plenty of diamonds on sale
over there, if you know the right people.'

I knew I needed to find out more, but I tried not to sound too
inquisitive. 'What a good idea. And he sold them here? Did he
just walk into a jeweller's and sell them?'

She shook her head. 'Not these diamonds. There's a man at
the station who buys them.' Realising that she had probably said
too much, she turned towards the door. 'Anyway, I need to get on.
The theatre will be open to the public in a few days' time and
everything's got to be sparkling clean.'

I shook her hand and wished her a safe journey, hoping that
she really would be able to achieve her dream of getting to the
UK but knowing that it wouldn't be easy. After the door had
closed behind her, I sat down and reflected on what I'd just

heard. Could diamonds form a link between two murdered asylum seekers, a pair of Dutch jewellers with a 'gentlemen's agreement,' and a bent police officer? The ramifications of this were potentially huge. And what had she meant when she'd said, 'Not these diamonds'?

It occurred to me that I maybe knew somebody who knew somebody who could help with this conundrum.

* * *

The first thing I did, after saying goodbye and good luck to Zebra, was to drive to an even more deserted part of the suburbs where there was nobody around. I parked in a patch of shade, pulled out my phone, and called Anna, who answered almost immediately.

'*Ciao*, Dan. Where are you?'

'In the van, thinking about taking Oscar for a good long walk, but first, I was wondering if you could give me the phone number of your friend in the tiger costume, Amy Mackintosh. She told me her husband's a geologist, and I need to speak to somebody who knows about diamonds.'

She gave me the number, and we agreed to carry on spending the nights out at my place in the hills, seeing as Florence was already getting uncomfortably warm. I told her I'd make a mixed salad and she sounded delighted – but maybe that was just because she wasn't going to have to do the cooking for a change.

I dialled Amy's number and was pleased to hear her voice. After a quick exchange of greetings, I asked her if it might be possible for me to speak to her husband about a geology matter. She laughed.

'Sandy's always happy to talk about geology. He's here with me now. I'll put him on.'

A few moments later, I heard a Scottish voice. 'Hello, Alexander Mackintosh here. How can I help?'

'Hello, Mr... Dr Mackintosh.' For all I knew, he might even be Professor Mackintosh. He was quick to reassure me.

'Just call me Sandy. Everybody else does. If I remember right, you're the Englishman married to an Italian who's lucky enough to live in Florence. Amy told me about your book launch last week. She's been reading it and is very enthusiastic about it. Apparently, I absolutely must read it after her. Congratulations.' He sounded very friendly.

'Hi, Sandy. Thanks for speaking to me and say thanks to Amy for investing in a copy of my book.' I decided not to specify that Anna and I weren't married as I moved on to the matter in hand. 'I gather from Amy that you're the man to speak to about diamonds. I know very little about them apart from them allegedly being a girl's best friend. Can you spare me a few minutes?'

'Of course, fire away.'

I gave him a quick summary of what Amélie had told me and asked him what she might have meant when she'd said, 'Not these diamonds'. He answered with a question.

'Did she say her brother-in-law had been working in the DRC?'

'Yes, and he and his wife are originally from the Central African Republic.'

'Then these are almost certainly conflict diamonds, sometimes called blood diamonds. Do those names ring a bell?'

'Yes, vaguely.'

He could tell from my uncertain tone that I needed help, so he launched into an explanation. 'There are certain parts of Africa where terrorists, criminals or armed militias have hijacked the diamond trade, and hundreds of thousands, probably millions, of people have had to flee their homes to escape the brutality of the unscrupulous people exploiting the mines. Places like Sierra Leone and the DRC have seen the worst of it. Although some of the proceeds go to criminals, lots of the money goes to rebel forces fighting supposedly legitimate governments, and that causes even more upheaval for the people over there. The diamonds mined under these circumstances have been given the name "conflict diamonds", for obvious reasons.'

This was fascinating. 'So what's the difference between conflict diamonds and ordinary diamonds?'

'As far as the stones themselves are concerned, none at all. They're all essentially just carbon crystals. The difference from a legal point of view is that the trade in conflict diamonds has been banned in many parts of the world, particularly Europe.'

'I see, but if they're the exact same stone, how can you tell the difference?'

'Regulators have been wrestling with that for years. There was a thing called the Kimberley Process set up a few years back and, although it's been massively abused, it sort of still operates. According to the KP, any diamond has to come with a certificate attesting to its place of origin. That way, the hope was that the warlords and the criminals wouldn't be able to sell their looted diamonds and they would run out of money pretty quickly.'

'From your tone, Sandy, I get the impression this maybe hasn't worked out quite as they hoped.'

'Exactly.' There was a frustrated note to his voice. 'The system has been abused from day one. Let's face it, if a bag of diamonds is mined by what is effectively slave labour at the hands of criminal overlords in the DRC or elsewhere, but then smuggled from there to, say, South Africa and declared as having been found in that country, the certificates are issued and no questions asked.

Or, at least, the questions are probably asked, but there's no way of proving that the diamonds aren't from South Africa.'

'So if this guy brought three conflict diamonds with him from the DRC, theoretically, he shouldn't have been able to sell them in Europe without certificates of origin?'

'And you're quite right – theoretically. That's where you need a trader who's prepared to bend the rules. After all, these diamonds are sold on the black market at a considerably lower price than legitimately mined ones, so there's a bigger profit to be made. What you've got to do now is to find that dodgy trader. Traditionally, Antwerp has always been the home of the diamond trade in Europe, but Italy has also been cashing in on the flood of diamonds smuggled over there, often by so-called asylum seekers coming over the Mediterranean from Libya.'

I felt a surge of satisfaction as the pieces of the jigsaw began to fall into place. 'That's fascinating, thanks a lot.'

He offered a suggestion. 'Seeing as it's Italy, might it be the Mafia?'

It was a sensible suggestion. 'I must admit that it wouldn't surprise me if they were involved, particularly when you consider that there are at least three or four different branches of organised crime still operating happily in Italy. I can well imagine that a supply of cheap diamonds would be welcomed by the Mafia, but in this case, I believe the police already know the identity of a couple of these rogue traders. Unfortunately for them, they've both just been murdered.'

'That's the other reason they're called blood diamonds. So much value in such a tiny item tends to bring out the worst in people.'

I thanked him warmly and put down the phone, catching Oscar's eye in the rear-view mirror. 'And now, old buddy, I think we've earned ourselves a long walk.'

18

WEDNESDAY AFTERNOON

When I got home, the first thing I did was to change into shorts and trainers and head off up the hill with Oscar, clutching the script for *Ultimatum* given to me by Zebra. It was, if anything, even warmer today than the previous days and we were soon hugging the shade. Up here in the hills to the south of Florence, there were wonderful views northwards towards the deep-green bulk of the Apennines and to the south into the rolling hills of the heart of Tuscany, but today I was concentrating my attention on the script, trying not to trip over as I walked and read at the same time.

Nevertheless, I couldn't miss the fact that spring was definitely in the air and there were green shoots and young leaves already appearing on the vines. As we walked past, lizards basking in the sun on the dry stone walls dashed for cover and I even spotted a hare disappearing into a clump of trees ahead of me. Luckily, Oscar didn't see it or he would have been after it like a shot. Determined to try and work off some of the food I'd been consuming over the past few days, I stuck the script back in my pocket and jogged several kilometres up the track to the top of the hill, where I stopped for a well-earned rest in the shade of a clump of cypress trees.

First things first, I pulled out my phone and called the mayor. He answered immediately and, from the echo, I got the impression he was in his car.

'*Ciao*, Dan. Any news?'

'*Ciao*, Ugo. Yes, I'm pleased to report that I now have the full name of your daughter's boyfriend. It's Tiberio Carbone.'

'Carbone?' He sounded surprised. 'Did you say Carbone?'

'That's right. Why, is something wrong?'

'No, not wrong, but I think I now know why Monica didn't want to introduce him to us.' He produced a noise that was hard to identify. I couldn't tell whether it was a snort or a laugh. 'I think I know who he is; in fact, I'm sure of it. He must be the son of the leader of the main opposition party on the town council. I heard that his boy was studying medicine, so that must be this Tiberio. I've crossed swords in the Palazzo Vecchio with his father, Umberto Carbone, on numerous occasions.' This time, I felt sure I could hear him laugh. 'How wonderfully Shakespearean! Monica was afraid that I might not approve of the son because I don't approve of the father. In fact, Umberto is a likeable and honourable man, even though his political views are diametrically opposite my own.'

'Does this mean you have no objections?'

'You must be joking, Dan. In this day and age, what a father thinks about his daughter's choice of friends counts for very little. Good luck to her, and if it becomes serious then that's fine with me. It could be useful to have a medic in the family. Of course, the problem I now have is what do I do? If I tell her that I know who he is and I'm quite happy about it, she's sure to ask me how I found out who he is. If she knows that I hired a private investigator, she'll probably go crazy – and I wouldn't blame her. What would you do?' He sounded genuinely troubled.

I thought about it for a moment or two before a solution presented itself. 'If you and your wife are going to see the play she's in on Saturday, you'll see Tiberio in the lead role. I've been bullied into agreeing to play a minor role in the play myself, so I could always ask the director to introduce him to you if your daughter doesn't. You then say, "Carbone? I don't suppose your father is my good friend Umberto, by any chance?" How about that?'

That suggestion met with immediate approval and Ugo was sounding a happy man by the end of the call.

My mind returned to diamonds, and I tried calling Virgilio again. I had already tried phoning him to tell him what I'd learnt from Amélie and then from Sandy Mackintosh, but there was still no answer and I left a message asking him to give me an urgent call. I then spent the next twenty or thirty minutes leafing through the typewritten pages of the script, marking the lines spoken by my character, Cesare. I also took a good look at the stage directions, but I knew I'd have to get Zebra to go through that sort of thing with me in the morning.

By the end of it, I was feeling slightly reassured – but only slightly. There were probably no more than a hundred words altogether spoken by my character, but often the lines consisted of barely two or three words each, so my problem was not so much remembering my lines as remembering when to utter them. Ever since agreeing to do this for Zebra, I'd been regretting it, but, as she had said, the die had now been cast and I just had to get on with it.

I was interrupted by Virgilio calling me back. I started by asking him if he'd been able to give Luuc Berg a full interview. The answer was not yet.

'I've been tied up all afternoon and I only got around to calling the villa a short while ago. I spoke to his sister, who told me Luuc's spending the afternoon at the Uffizi gallery – on his own as usual – and she can't contact him. She says he's probably turned off his phone. I've left a message with her to say that I'll go there at nine o'clock tomorrow morning to speak to him. I asked her about his movements and, in effect, he has no alibi for either of the murders or, indeed, for when Marco was knocked down, although none of the three Berg family vehicles have a scratch on them. She said he'd told her he left the Netherlands on Friday afternoon and stopped at a hotel in the French Alps late that night before setting off again early on Saturday morning – about five or six hours' drive from here – but she didn't know where the hotel was. Apparently, he arrived in Florence at lunchtime on Saturday and they all met up for lunch in town before going to their father's villa. As for last night between ten and midnight, she said he was out walking around the town, and she had no idea where he went. Reading between the lines, I get the impression that there's maybe a bit of a family rift going on.'

'Mm, I wonder what might be behind that. Hopefully, the French hotel will have a record of him and he should be able to produce motorway or fuel receipts to back up his story. Mind you, if he can't, the fact that he doesn't have an alibi doesn't necessarily imply culpability. In fact, considering how professionally the murders of the two Dutchmen were carried out, the fact that he hasn't got a clear-cut alibi is actually in his favour. Surely a pro would have organised that in advance.'

Virgilio was still suspicious. 'Luuc Berg is a tall, strong man who fits the CCTV imagery we have for both murders. He could easily have killed his father and/or Jacobs. Maybe he killed his father in revenge for dumping their mother and then he went after Jacobs for the sake of a box of gemstones.'

'And Marco? Did Luuc set out to kill him as well and, if so, why, and in what vehicle?'

'Maybe he rented a car...' Virgilio was clutching at straws and both of us knew that. What possible reason could Luuc have had to want to kill Marco?

I added another query. 'Besides, how did Luuc know about the diamonds in the box? You didn't give the family any specific details of the contents of the safe or mention a connection with Jacobs, did you?'

'Maybe his father said something to the housekeeper, who passed it on...'

I could hear that Virgilio was sounding less and less convinced so I offered my alternative theory in the hope of cheering him up. 'Try this for size. I think I might have managed to find the missing link connecting Berg, Jacobs and the two *extra-comunitari* – and, by extension, the traitor in the Florence police force.'

I went on to tell him what I'd learned this afternoon. 'So how about this as a scenario? David Berg has a regular deal going with somebody – probably an asylum seeker – at the main station. The man at the station buys smuggled gemstones from other asylum seekers on Berg's behalf and passes them on in return for a fee. When Berg has a fair collection of them – like a cigar boxful, for example – he sells them on to his friend Jacobs.'

Virgilio grunted approvingly. 'That would explain the deaths of the Africans. They were killed for the diamonds they were carrying.'

I carried on. 'Exactly. However, somebody gets wind of what's going on and decides to take over the operation. He manages to make one or both of the asylum seekers at the station talk before stabbing them to death – and discovers Berg's name. I would think the last man to be stabbed is likely to have been Berg's buyer and it was he who gave away the Dutchman's name. This somebody waits for Berg outside his shop on the Ponte Vecchio on Friday night, bustles him inside and tries to get him to hand over all the diamonds – little realising that they're in the safe at the villa. Unfortunately, in the course of the interrogation, the old man dies, leaving our perpetrator with the problem of what to do with the body. He knows any competent pathologist will see that it was murder so he tries to make it look like suicide, but doesn't quite get it right.'

Virgilio was sounding more and more enthusiastic. 'Terrific, Dan, that sounds very plausible, but how did the murderer then find out about Axel Jacobs, assuming his death is the work of the same killer? The only people to establish a clear link between the two deaths so far are us, and the police report is highly confidential. This almost certainly implies inside knowledge – somebody in the police, no doubt the person who's been destroying the files – doesn't it?'

I decided to play devil's advocate – even if I didn't really believe it myself. 'I suppose that's the likely conclusion, but not necessarily. What if Berg, in an attempt to misdirect his assailant on Friday night, told him that the diamonds were with Jacobs? And what if that assailant was Luuc Berg? I'm not convinced, but it's a possibility.'

'I sincerely hope you're right, Dan, but I fear in my bones that somewhere in the Florence police force, there's somebody who has murdered not only the two asylum seekers but also a pair of Dutch jewellers and has attempted to murder Marco. That means I'm working with a serial killer. It's a scary and a very distasteful thought.'

'I'm afraid that's probably right. It looks most likely that it was somebody on your force who was able to access the Berg file – and any senior officer could have done that – and from that, he must have picked up on the fact that Jacobs was also in on it. Don't forget that Jacobs was killed the night before the safe was opened, so the killer may well have hoped to find that Jacobs had the diamonds. Maybe the murderer went to his hotel room hoping to get his hands on either the cigar box of diamonds or the three hundred thousand euros, unaware that these were in the safe all along. Jacobs wasn't a big, strong man, but he struck me as the sort of tough character who would try to stand up for himself, and that would explain the bruises on his body. Our killer maybe didn't mean to murder him at first, but he just squeezed a bit too hard. What do you think?'

'I think that's almost certainly the way it went, Dan, although I suppose we should still keep Luuc Berg in the frame just in case. Let's see what he says when I interview him tomorrow. So we currently have four potential suspects, but no proof against any of them.' The frustration in his voice was clear to hear.

'Any joy with CCTV or dashcam footage of Marco's accident?'

'Tech are going through it now. They say that they have footage from a number of sources, but nothing showing the moment of the accident itself. They're still looking, and I'm on my way back to the *questura* right now. If we spot anything, I'll give you a call.'

When the call ended, Oscar and I picked up our walk again, following a curving route that would eventually bring us back to my house. As we came back down the hill again, my phone started ringing. I didn't recognise the number so I answered cautiously.

'Pronto.'

'Signor Armstrong?' It was a man's voice, speaking Italian. 'My name is Inspector Faldo of the Florence police and I'm investigating the murder of a Dutch citizen, name of Jacobs. I understand from Commissario Pisano that Axel Jacobs came to see you on Monday. I wonder if you'd be able to drop into the *questura* to give me a statement of what was said.' He sounded very polite. 'I would be very grateful.'

I glanced at my watch. It was half past four. Although I'd promised to prepare dinner tonight, I knew that this was a golden opportunity to sit down and talk to one of the main suspects. 'I'm just out in the country at the moment. Give me time to change and I should be able to get there in an hour or so. Would five-thirty be okay with you?'

After a quick shower, a change of clothes, and an apologetic call to Anna about the lack of an evening meal, I managed to get to the police station through the late-afternoon traffic at just after five-thirty. The officer at the front desk knew me and Oscar by now and directed me upstairs to Inspector Faldo's office on the second floor. Like the other floors, this was open-plan and I found his desk at the far end. I recognised him from his photos on social media, but I feigned ignorance and asked a female officer sitting near the door if she could point me at him. She very kindly accompanied me to his desk and left me there. He looked up and gave me a friendly smile.

'Signor Armstrong, thank you for coming. Do take a seat. Can I get you a coffee?'

He was a fit-looking man with broad shoulders, but close up, there were lines on his face and he looked older than in his photos online, all of his forty-one years. Of course, I reminded myself, I had only seen him in happy holiday snaps so far, and now he was on duty and trying to pick up the pieces of a murder investigation that was all new to him.

I thanked him for the offer of coffee but refused. He immediately started his questions.

'This shouldn't take long but I'm interested to hear what you and Jacobs discussed and to get your impression of him.'

I rattled off a summary of Monday morning's meeting with Jacobs and I saw Faldo take notes. Every now and then, he shot me a question and by the end of our session, I had got the impression that he was a good, professional police officer. He thanked me and sat back.

'As you may know, I've only been involved in this case since Inspector Innocenti had that unfortunate accident yesterday. Could you tell me what you thought of Jacobs? Do you think he might have murdered David Berg?'

'I very much doubt it. Although Berg was about ten years older than him, Jacobs was seventy-six and he wasn't a particularly big man. I'm not sure he would have had the strength to murder Berg and then, more particularly, to carry his body to the edge of the bridge and push him over the side. Also, isn't it a bit strange that he would kill Berg and then come to me about it?'

He nodded. 'I suppose so. And what about his story of giving three hundred thousand euros to Berg in exchange for a cigar box? Do you believe that?'

I realised that this probably indicated that Virgilio hadn't told him about the contents of the safe yet so I stayed vague. 'He sounded convincing enough, but I suppose it all depends on whether the cigar box is ever found – if it ever existed – and what's inside it. Of course, the box might have been in Jacobs's room last night and the murderer took it and whatever was in it.' I kept a close eye on his face but didn't see anything untoward. 'Can I ask if you've made any progress in identifying the murderer? I imagine a hotel like the Grand must have CCTV.' I thought it wiser to distance myself from the investigation.

'Not as far as I'm aware, I'm afraid.'

Seeing as he had been at the hotel interviewing people today, I thought this was disingenuous. There was no way he couldn't have known about the CCTV and, seeing as the images had already been sent to Virgilio, they would surely have also been available to him. Of course, as I knew only too well, in a murder investigation, it was never good to broadcast information to any Tom, Dick or Harry – or, indeed, Dan – so maybe he was just being cautious. What was interesting was that he was able to give me the lie without blinking. Clearly, he was an accomplished liar, and I made a mental note of that. If he could lie about one thing, he could lie about other things. I tried another tack.

'And what about Marco's accident? Do you think that's all it was, or was he deliberately targeted?'

He reached down and ostentatiously closed his notebook. 'Our investigations are still ongoing. Thank you very much, Signor Armstrong, for coming in. I'm very grateful.'

I could take a hint so I stood up, shook his hand, and left, with Oscar trotting along behind me.

When I got out to the stairs, who should I meet coming down towards me but Superintendent Vincenzo Grande. I could see from his face that he'd recognised me and he stopped to shake my hand.

'Signor Armstrong, isn't it? I remember meeting you when there was that awful business out at the golf course a year or two ago. Commissario Pisano always speaks very highly of you.'

I decided to take this opportunity to talk to the man as much as I could. His Sicilian accent had softened slightly since I had last seen him, and I found him easier to understand – although I'm a fine one to talk when it comes to dodgy Italian accents.

'Virgilio's very kind. In fact, I'm just going up to talk to him now to see if he's interested in a game of tennis some time. Do you play?'

He shook his head and smiled. 'No, tennis is definitely not my game.' He patted his stomach. 'Maybe ten years ago...'

'You look as if you get out a lot. What's your sport?'

'I'm a hunter.' He winked at me. 'And I'm not just talking about criminals. Wild boar, ducks, geese, I just enjoy being out in the fresh air.'

As we were speaking, I was surreptitiously studying him. Although I couldn't see him choosing to dress in a hoodie in normal, everyday life, he was tall enough to fit the profile of the man in the CCTV footage. Could it be that Vincenzo Grande was our serial killer? He was positively exuding bonhomie, but that didn't prove anything. I remembered one particularly nasty killer, responsible for the deaths of three women in London, who had had a permanent smile on his face every time I'd seen him, including as the cuffs were fitted to his wrists and he was led away.

He glanced at his watch and held out his hand to shake mine again. 'I'm afraid I must be off. I have an appointment.'

I said goodbye and made my way to Virgilio's office, where I found him staring at his laptop. He looked up when I came in.

'*Ciao*, Dan, this is a pleasant surprise.'

I explained that I'd been summoned by Inspector Faldo to give him my statement about Jacobs, and Virgilio got up and went over to make sure the door was closed. He came back to his seat and leant over the desk towards me. 'What did you think of him?'

'Very professional. He was polite and thorough. Certainly, no obvious signs of guilt, although – like a few politicians I could name – he has the ability to look you straight in the eye and lie through his teeth. This is not necessarily suspicious in itself, but it's worth bearing in mind. I gather you haven't told him about the contents of the safe yet. I pleaded ignorance. When are you going to tell him?'

'I'm going to add the latest developments to the file this evening.'

Something Faldo had said came back to me. 'Tell me, does the existing version of the file mention a cigar box? Faldo knew about it and I was wondering if that might be suspicious.'

His answer was disappointing. 'It mentions a cigar box containing unspecified valuables worth three hundred thousand euros but it doesn't go into detail. I'll reveal what we found in the safe when I write up the report this evening.'

'Bang goes another great idea. I thought for a moment this might indicate Faldo knew more than he should. Ah, well...'

Virgilio gave a weary smile and pointed to his computer. 'Changing the subject to Marco, I've just been sent this by Tech. They've been studying doorbell footage and some dashcam footage around the time that Marco was run down. See what you think.'

I spent several minutes flicking through the various video clips, but without seeing anything significant. Twenty or thirty vehicles had gone down Marco's road around the time that he'd been hit and, infuriatingly, none of the cameras had been able to give a clear shot of the faces of any of the drivers. Even more annoyingly, only three or four number plates were visible. All the others had been hidden by passing cars, trees, cyclists or delivery vans. I looked up at Virgilio and shook my head sadly. 'There's nothing there that leaps out of the screen at us, is there?'

'No, not a thing.'

The phone rang and Virgilio answered it. It was a very quick conversation and when he replaced the receiver, there was a smile on his face. 'That's a bit of luck. The *vice questore* wants to speak to me about a different matter. He's on his way down here now. I can introduce you as our friendly local interpreter. You already know Superintendent Grande and now you've met Faldo and Luuc Berg, so this way you will, at least, get a look at all of our main suspects.'

While we waited, I told him about my brief conversation with the superintendent on the stairs, and he asked me if I thought he could be our killer. All I could tell him in response was that anything was possible.

A couple of minutes later, the door opened and the *vice questore* strode in. Giuseppe Verdi was impeccably turned out in a grey Prince of Wales check suit, white shirt, and what looked suspiciously like a red and blue striped Brigade of Guards tie. Considering that we were in Italy, I considered that highly unlikely, but with his well-trimmed moustache and polished shoes, he looked more like a retired British general than either of the two retired generals I'd come across in the course of my career at the Met. He shot me an uncertain glance but then stopped dead when Oscar stirred and pulled himself to his feet, tail wagging in welcome – but the reaction of the *vice questore* was far from welcoming.

'What's this animal doing in here, Pisano? This is a police station, not a zoo.' Even his speech was clipped and formal, like his appearance. He looked outraged and, me being me, I felt slighted on my dog's behalf. I've never liked people who throw their weight about and I took an instant dislike to this autocratic character with the composer's name. For his part, Oscar glanced up at me with his *what's his problem?* expression. I was quick to improvise.

'I'm just leaving. This is a trainee sniffer dog.'

'What kind of sniffer dog?' He gave Oscar the sort of look people give to something on the underside of their shoe.

As Oscar's nose was only a couple of feet from the *vice questore*'s crotch, I had to struggle to keep a straight face as I replied. 'Suspicious substances, sir. Anything from drugs to explosives. I don't suppose you have anything explosive in your trousers, do you?' I glanced across at Virgilio and saw him grin and duck behind the shelter of the laptop screen.

Giuseppe Verdi's face changed to a glowing, pillar-box-red colour so rapidly that it looked as though he might be about to explode – with or without the assistance of my imaginary sniffer dog – so I decided the time was right for Oscar and me to depart.

I knew how I was going to be spending my evening – learning my lines.

19

THURSDAY MORNING

Thursday was my day for having ideas – not all of them outstanding.

Oscar and I were halfway up the gravel track behind my house on our early-morning walk next day when I had my first idea. Credit where credit's due, I had Oscar to thank for this. I had been thinking about Virgilio's problem of how to catch the killer without being able to draw upon the full resources of the Florence police. As long as three of the four possible suspects were members of the force, everything had to be kept strictly on a restricted 'need-to-know' basis. I was turning over in my head various possible ways of helping the investigation along when Oscar helped me find a solution.

We were approaching a corner where the track curves around the top of one of my neighbours' olive groves when Oscar deposited yet another stick at my feet for me to throw for him. Although he's never received any gun-dog training – as I had told the gentlemen at the wildfowl lake – he's certainly inherited the retriever gene and his idea of fun is chasing after sticks and pine cones that I throw for him as we walk and bringing them back to me. I threw this particular stick for him but, when it landed, it skidded across the track and wedged itself between two large stones at the foot of a wall. Oscar galloped after it and, after unsuccessfully trying to drag it out with his teeth, set about digging it out with his front paws, sending the white gravel flying in all directions, glistening in the morning sun as it did so. It was at that moment that it occurred to me that a good way for Virgilio to flush out the perpetrator would be to set a trap.

My industrious dog finally managed to wrench the stick out of the wall and dropped it proudly at my feet. I took it and threw it into the olive grove on the other side of the track for him to fetch while I squatted down, lifted a handful of the irregular pieces of gravel and let them run through my fingers onto the track. They weren't diamonds, but they would do. I removed one of Oscar's poo bags from my pocket and filled it with gravel until I reckoned I had at least the same weight as the diamonds in the cigar box. I then perched on the wall and called Virgilio.

'*Ciao*, Virgilio, any developments?'

'*Ciao*, Dan. Some promising news from the hospital. Marco's beginning to remember things that happened on the afternoon of the so-called accident. Before you ask, no, he can't remember the phone call yet, but the medics say this is a very good sign. What about you? Any bright ideas?'

'Maybe. Did you file your report of the latest developments in the Berg case last night like you said? If so, what did you say about the contents of the safe?'

'Yes, it's on file now. I indicated that the technician managed to open the safe and I made reference to the provisions of the old man's will, but I didn't itemise all the contents of the safe. Forensics are doing that.'

'So it's now common knowledge that there was a cigar box full of diamonds?'

'No, I had already mentioned the cigar box, but I just said it was in there and it contained items of considerable value allegedly belonging to Axel Jacobs. But that isn't common knowledge to everybody in the *questura*, only to people with access to the file – and that definitely includes our three suspects. Why do you ask?'

'I reckon I might have come up with a way of setting a trap. What time did you say you're going to see Luuc Berg this morning?'

'Nine. Do you want to tag along?'

'That would be good, yes, thanks, but I need to sit down and talk to you first to see what you think of my idea. Why don't we meet up somewhere before nine so I can go through what I've been thinking?'

Before going to meet Virgilio, I loaded what Anna calls my 'bag of tricks' into the van. This is a small case in which I keep mainly electronic surveillance equipment, ranging from tracking devices to spy cameras and voice-activated eavesdropping recorders.

Virgilio and I met up in the car park of a supermarket on the outskirts of Signa and parked side by side in a remote corner. He came and joined me in my van, stretching his arm back to ruffle Oscar's ears and dissuade him from climbing over the back of the rear seat. After he had suitably greeted my dog, he turned back towards me and raised an inquisitive eyebrow.

'Well, what's this plan of yours?'

Ever since the first spark of an idea had occurred to me, I'd been turning this over in my head. It wasn't perfect, but it might do the trick.

'This is principally aimed at the three police suspects, but seeing as we're talking to Luuc Berg this morning, maybe we can extend it to him as well.' I pulled out the bag of gravel and handed it to him. 'Without opening the top of the cigar box, it's impossible to tell whether it's full of diamonds or gravel, right?' He nodded and I continued. 'What I'm suggesting is that we open the safe, take the diamonds out of the box, put them into a bag and leave them there. Then we refill the cigar box with gravel. Like I say, for anybody who sees the closed box, who's to say what's inside it?'

He nodded. 'Okay, I get that, but what are you planning on doing with the box of fake diamonds?'

'I suggest you stick it in a clear evidence bag so it's easily identified and take it back to your office. Somehow or other, it will then be up to you to make sure that the three prime suspects are aware that you've got it. Faldo will be easy enough because he's already been assigned to the case. Superintendent Grande is your superior officer so it would be normal for you to report to him, and you could maybe ask him to inform the *vice questore*. By the way, I hope you didn't mind my having a go at him yesterday, but he got on my nerves. I rather hope he turns out to be the killer. I really didn't like the man.'

Virgilio laughed. 'I almost choked myself trying not to laugh. After you'd left, he queried which branch of the force you were from – quite probably so he could put in a complaint for impertinence to a superior officer – and I told him that you were from outside the force, something to do with the Protezione degli Animali. Anyway, go on with your plan.'

'I've brought a selection of surveillance devices with me and what I would suggest is that you take the box of gravel back to the *questura* and make sure that the suspects know that you've locked it into one of the drawers of your desk. I've seen your desk. It was probably made thirty or forty years ago and the locks should be very easy to pick or to force. I'll set up a couple of cameras in your office and then we sit back and wait to see what happens.'

Virgilio took his time before replying. When he did, there was caution in his voice. 'I think it's worth a go, but I seriously doubt whether our killer would take the chance of exposing his identity by removing such valuable evidence. After all, my office could only be accessed by a serving officer and he'd know that by stealing evidence, he'd immediately start a witch hunt. Let's try it, by all means, and I hope it works, but my feeling is that the killer has acted very professionally so far and I doubt whether he'd be prepared to take such a risk now.'

'I know what you mean, but he's almost certainly already killed the two Dutchmen, plus probably the two asylum seekers, so as to get his hands on the contents of that cigar box. Maybe he desperately needs the money. Given that it seems very likely that he tried to kill Marco, this means that he knows we're onto him and it'll only be a matter of time before the noose tightens around him. What if he's decided to make a run for it before we catch up with him? Three hundred thou would be a nice little nest egg to help him start a new life somewhere a long way away. I'm certainly not suggesting that you give up the investigation in the meantime but, like you, I think it's worth a go.'

'And Luuc Berg, how do we involve him?'

'I've been thinking about that. Why don't you call him into your office and arrange to leave him alone with the box for a few minutes? You never know, he might succumb to temptation.'

'Okay, that's easy enough to do. I'll ask him if he minds dropping in to see me later today. I'm sure I can invent a suitable excuse – like trying to identify a photo or some such.' He glanced at his watch. 'Right, shall we go up to the villa now?'

I followed him up the road to David Berg's villa and parked alongside his car. Ines opened the front door to us and we went upstairs to Berg's study. We broke the police seal on the door, went in and closed the door behind us, pulling on disposable gloves, even though Forensics had already been through the contents of the safe with a fine-tooth comb. While Virgilio opened the safe, I took out the bag of gravel and emptied it onto a sheet of newspaper. He brought the cigar box over to the desk and carefully tipped the precious contents onto a clean sheet of paper. We then both took it in turns to weigh the diamonds in one hand and empty some of the gravel from my little bag in the other until we reckoned they were roughly equal. He then poured the diamonds into another bag and locked them securely back in the safe again. While he was doing that, I filled the cigar box with the gravel, squeezed it into a transparent evidence bag, sealed it, and handed it to Virgilio.

'I would suggest you make sure Luuc sees the box, but don't tell him what's in it. If he starts talking about diamonds, that might be a step in the right direction, although, let's face it, to be worth three hundred thousand in gold, it's pretty obvious it has to be precious stones of some kind or maybe a different rare metal at a push.'

He nodded. 'We can but try.'

When we went back downstairs again, we found Emma Berg and her brother waiting in the hall for us. Casper shook hands with us while his sister made a fuss of Oscar.

'Good morning, gentlemen. I have a message for you from my brother, Luuc.' Casper sounded irritated – either with us or with his brother. 'You were expecting to see him here at nine, weren't you? Well, his message was, and I quote, "I've never been to Florence before and I've got better things to do with my time. Tell the police I can see them between eleven and twelve but I'm booked for a tour of the Basilica of Santa Croce at nine-thirty, and I'm climbing Brunelleschi's dome at one." He said he'll leave his phone on mute so he can be contacted by text.' Casper shook his head slowly. 'I must apologise for my brother's rudeness. I'm afraid he's always had an awkward streak.'

Virgilio and I exchanged glances. This actually suited us better as it would solve the problem of how to get Luuc into the *questura*. Virgilio thanked Casper for passing on the message and asked him if he would be kind enough to send a text to his brother, asking him to report to the *questura* as soon after eleven as he could.

I followed Virgilio into Florence and parked outside the *questura*, where he surreptitiously pointed out the cars belonging to the three suspects. All three were a whole lot newer and cleaner than my van and, again, I found myself wondering how their owners could afford their respective lifestyles – particularly Inspector Faldo, as his salary was the lowest of the three.

Upstairs, I wasted no time in setting the trap, concealing two tiny cameras – each little bigger than a cherry – pointing towards the desk from different directions. I hid one among files on a shelf with the other peeking out of the folds of a scarf abandoned on top of a filing cabinet since winter. Virgilio set the cigar box down on his desk and made a phone call.

'Hello, Superintendent Grande, I've just got back from the Berg villa and I thought it might be useful to give you and Faldo a summary of how far we've got with the investigation. Could you spare me a few minutes?'

When he set the phone down, he was smiling. 'Excellent! Grande told me that the *vice questore* has been asking about the Berg case and he's going to see if he can get him to come along for my briefing as well. That way, I can get all three of them together.' He indicated Oscar, who was very interested in something in Virgilio's waste bin. 'You'd better clear off and take your four-legged friend with you. Verdi will blow a gasket if he sees him in here again.'

'Right, I'm off. Good luck.'

20

THURSDAY MORNING/AFTERNOON

I left the *questura* and headed out to the Teatro Dell'Arno for my session with Zebra. As usual, Oscar was delighted to see her and he sat on her lap all the way through almost an hour of rehearsal. Considering that he weighs over fifty pounds, this spoke volumes about her strength – not just her ability to raise her arms with the weight of jewellery attached to them. As a director, she was very patient and she had a way of explaining remarkably clearly what I had to do and where I had to go, as well as how I should look and act. By the end of the session, I was exhausted, but I got the impression that she was reassured, although I was still nervous. After all, the opening night was in little more than forty-eight hours' time.

I drove back to my office and parked the van in the courtyard. Although it had been a glorious sunny morning so far, I could see rainclouds gathering and I found myself smiling. The tourists might not like the rain, but I knew that all the farmers around here would be only too pleased. Tuscany has been getting drier and drier over the course of the last decade and rain has become a rare and precious commodity.

Upstairs in the office, I found Lina looking and sounding more cheerful. I told her I'd been with Virgilio and that he'd also been sounding much more like his normal self. I didn't tell her that our chances of laying our hands on a serial killer relied on the murderer being stupid – or desperate – enough to fall for my gravel-in-a-box trick or for Marco to fully recover his memory and tell us who had run him down – or at least who had phoned him just before the accident.

I went into my office and spent the remainder of the morning catching up on admin that I'd been neglecting until there was a call from Virgilio just after midday.

'*Ciao*, Dan. I thought you'd like to know that the first part of your plan has been put into operation. I had Verdi, Grande and Faldo in my office for a briefing and I made sure they had a good look at the cigar box before I locked it in my desk drawer. None of them commented on it very much, which struck me as a bit strange – after all, it's not as if I smoke cigars – but then I told them that it had come from Berg's safe and its contents are valuable. I said I couldn't take it out of the evidence bag and show them what was inside because Forensics still had work to do on it. Interestingly, Superintendent Grande asked me if there was gold in the box and I shook it so they could hear the gravel rattling about before announcing that it contained a quantity of precious stones. If he already knew that there were diamonds in there, maybe he was just doing a bit of disinformation, pretending that this was all new to him. Neither of the other two commented but I could tell that both of them were interested – for the right reasons or the wrong reasons, I've no way of knowing.'

'And what about Luuc Berg? I trust he showed up.'

'Yes, he's just left now. He was uncommunicative and unhelpful and, to all intents and purposes, uninterested. I told him that his father had left a lot of valuable items in the safe and that this box was only a small part of it. He just nodded and didn't comment. Coincidentally, while I was talking to him, I got a call from the front desk to say that a parcel had arrived for me, so I jumped at the excuse, murmured a quick apology, and left him there with the box in the evidence bag on the desk in front of him for three or four minutes while I went down to pick up the birthday present for Lina that I'd ordered online. It's a tennis racket, in case you're wondering.'

'And Luuc and the cigar box were still there?'

'Yes, and, as far as I could tell, untouched.'

'I'll drop by later on to check the camera footage with the app on my phone. What did you think of Luuc? Do you think he might be our killer? Obviously, he can't have anything to do with the missing files at the *questura*, but maybe he really did kill his father.'

'I'm not so sure. Yes, like his brother said, he's an awkward so-and-so, but do I see him as a murderer? No, I don't. Also, he produced a receipt for a hotel room in Modane, France, for Friday night. I haven't checked with the hotel yet and it could be a forgery or he might have paid and then not slept in it, but I must admit that I'm tending to rule him out as a serious suspect. You never know, the hotel may have CCTV footage that proves he was there.'

Mention of CCTV stirred something that had been bubbling away at the back of my mind ever since I had seen those photos of the hooded figure who had murdered Jacobs. 'You know the CCTV footage of the Grand Hotel? There were shots of the killer in the corridor and at Jacobs's door as well as when he left the hotel, but there was no sign of him arriving. Might this mean that he was staying there?'

'I got Faldo to check all the guests and he says none of them fitted the profile of the killer.'

'I see. What about dinner guests? There's a Michelin-starred restaurant there, after all. Could it have been one of the diners? Maybe the guy came in dressed normally and had dinner, then at ten o'clock, he slipped out to the toilets, changed into his black hoodie and did the deed. Presumably, there are CCTV cameras in the dining room. It might be worth checking to see if there was a lone diner there.'

'I can't remember seeing footage from the dining room, so I'll check it out. Good idea.'

'So what happens now?'

'Seeing as I need to leave my office unguarded for a few hours in the hope that one of our suspects will come sniffing around, I'm going to the tennis club for a light lunch and then I've booked a lesson with Gilberto at two to try and sort out my backhand. If you've got nothing better to do, why not come and join me at three, and I'll give you a game before we go back to check if any of our fish have taken the bait?'

'As long as it doesn't start raining, that sounds like a great idea. See you later.'

I then did a very silly thing.

As I put the phone down, my sleeve caught the cup of coffee Lina had brought me and tipped it into my lap. Fortunately, it was no longer boiling hot, but it made a real mess of my trousers. Although I had clothes at Anna's house, there was no parking anywhere near her place and I had no intention of walking through the crowded streets looking as if I'd wet myself – or worse – so I piled Oscar into the van and drove back to my house in the hills to change. When I got there, I changed into shorts and trainers, had a sandwich, and gave Oscar his lunch before deciding to take him for a quick walk before the rain started. The sky had been getting steadily darker and I knew it wouldn't be long. Somehow, I had a feeling Virgilio and I wouldn't be playing tennis this afternoon.

I headed up the track, playing fetch with Oscar as I walked and reading my lines out loud from the script while trying to look where I was going. As we reached a particularly steep part of the hillside, I heard the noise of a powerful engine coming up the track behind me. I called Oscar to my side and stepped into the undergrowth to let the vehicle pass. A dust-covered Land Rover appeared around the corner below us with a couple of bearded 4 x 4 aficionados inside. The vehicle had been kitted out as if it were about to embark on the Paris to Dakar off-road race with a winch on the front, an exhaust extension that rose up from the engine to almost the height of the vehicle and some of the chunkiest tyres I'd ever seen. These guys definitely wanted to look the part, even if they were just driving up a gravel track.

They gave me a casual wave as they passed but didn't slow down and they left Oscar and me sneezing in the dust cloud in their wake. As I stood there coughing and cursing, watching them disappear up the track and around a corner above us, I had my next brainwave of the day.

Something felt familiar and it took me a few moments to work out what it was before it came to me. I sat down on a stone wall, reached for my phone and went onto Facebook, where I located the pages belonging to Inspector Faldo's kids. It didn't take me long to find what I was looking for. I could remember seeing a photo of Faldo driving up a steep slope in a Land Rover, not dissimilar to the vehicle that had just smothered us in dust – but it was the background to the photo that interested me. I studied it carefully and blew it up to see if my memory had served me well.

It had.

There, at the top of the photo, was something I recognised. It was unmistakably the dilapidated old tower down by the wild-fowl lake. The photo must have been taken at the off-road driving centre in the old sand quarry on the far side of the lake. As I studied the photo, the idea that had sprung into my head crystallised. The fact that none of the vehicles belonging to our three police suspects or Luuc Berg had displayed any damage implied that if Marco's would-be murderer had indeed been one of them, he must have used another vehicle.

Like a battered Land Rover, for example.

I did my best to recall the video footage I'd seen of the vehicles passing near to the scene of Marco's accident and I had a feeling that there might have been a Land Rover among them. Virgilio would be able to check. The question was whether this had been one of the vehicles I'd seen outside the off-road centre and if the damage was still visible and, more importantly, whether there was still any DNA or other evidence to be seen. With rain on the way, somebody needed to get out there fast to investigate.

As I called Virgilio, I checked the time and saw that it was almost half past two and the phone rang and rang before going to voicemail. It suddenly occurred to me that he was having his tennis lesson at this very moment and he would be impossible to contact until three. When I heard the beep, I made a quick decision and left a message.

'Hi, Virgilio, it's just occurred to me that Faldo might have used one of the off-road vehicles from the 4 x 4 club near the wildfowl lake to try to murder Marco. Alternatively, maybe it was Superintendent Grande, whose shooting club is only about five hundred metres away from there. Either way, I need to check the vehicles there for damage before the rain comes and washes any evidence away. I'm going to go there now because I can't think of anybody else at the *questura* I can trust to help me. When you get this message, if I haven't called you again, please could you come out to the 4 x 4 centre with some DNA swabs and some evidence bags? Thanks.'

I called Oscar and ran back down the track to my house. The sky was getting ever darker so, without stopping to change out of my shorts, I jumped into the van with him and set off downhill as fast as I could.

It was just after three when I skidded to a halt at the turn-off to the wildfowl lake and took a left fork down a dusty track signposted *4 x 4 Centre*. This track curled sharply downwards into what had clearly once been a fairly sizeable old quarry. There was a muddy pond in the middle with vehicle tracks leading in and out of it, and those same tracks climbed and descended a series of obstacles ranging from heaps of earth and rocks to a near-vertical slope leading up and out of the quarry again. Over to the right was the wooden construction I had spotted before. This was obviously the clubhouse, but it was on a far smaller scale than the one for the hunters at the wildfowl lake. I parked alongside it and went over to the door but found it locked. A notice on the wall alongside the door indicated the opening hours and I saw that on Tuesdays and Thursdays, the centre was closed. This actually suited me perfectly as it meant there would be nobody here to wonder why I was snooping around their vehicles. I walked around the wooden hut but saw nobody. What I did see, however, were half a dozen off-road vehicles parked behind the building.

While Oscar wandered around, investigating the quarry, I set about the task of investigating the collection of fairly battered vehicles. Four of them were Land Rovers – clearly the vehicle of choice for the dedicated off-roader – and the other two were different makes. All of them, apart from having various dents and scratches and a liberal coating of dust, were shod with chunky tyres to help them over uneven terrain. I started with the Land Rovers. These all had a hefty steel front bumper running right across from side to side, and I could see that the front of this type of vehicle was effectively upright. I remembered reading an article years ago describing Land Rovers as having 'brick-like aerodynamics' and what this also meant, of course, was that in the event of an accident, particularly involving a pedestrian, the victim's body would take the full force of the vehicle rather than sliding up a sloping bonnet and avoiding the worst of the impact. From the severity of Marco's injuries, it could well be that he had been hit by one of these.

A cursory glance at the first one told me nothing. Yes, there were clumps of dry grass stuck in corners and multiple scratches, dents and bumps, but nothing immediately to indicate that this had been involved in a collision with a pedestrian. I knelt down and subjected the front of it to a close study but without seeing anything sinister. I did the same with the next Land Rover but, again, without success. When I transferred my attention to the third – by the look of it, at least twenty years old – my eye was drawn to the front of the vehicle on the driver's side. It was dented and there were two small, old-fashioned round lights, one orange – presumably, the indicator – and one a clear sidelight set into the aluminium bodywork. Both were cracked and the clear one was missing a piece. What was particularly interesting was the fact that on the remaining piece of plastic, I could see brown staining, which, on closer inspection, looked suspiciously like dried blood.

I pulled out my phone and took several photos of the vehicle with close-ups of the broken lights. I then used one of Oscar's useful poo bags to gradually work a piece of the stained plastic away from the broken light and drop it into the bag. I rolled this up and tucked it into my pocket before carrying on my inspection of the vehicle, finding other traces of blood and, in particular, a tiny piece of torn, grey material. From memory, the last few times I had seen Marco, he had been wearing grey trousers. This, too, went into a bag and into my pocket. As I completed my inspection, I felt a first heavy drop of rain on my head, immediately followed by more and more until, in a matter of seconds, it was absolutely bucketing down, and I was in imminent danger of getting soaked through.

Even Oscar, who loves water, was beginning to look bedraggled, so I straightened up and headed around to the front of the building and the shelter of my van. The once dusty ground had already turned to viscous mud, and I slipped and slid about as I walked, wondering who the driver of the Land Rover had been: Faldo or Grande. I was approaching my vehicle when I heard the sound of an engine and saw a dark-blue car coming gingerly down the bumpy track towards me, snaking from side to side in the slippery mud.

This was no 4 x 4. This was a very smart, shiny BMW saloon, and in the driving seat was none other than Inspector Roberto Faldo.

21

THURSDAY AFTERNOON

Inspector Faldo drove across the quarry floor until he reached me. He switched off the engine before climbing out into the torrential downpour. Apparently oblivious to the fact that his smart, light-grey suit jacket was rapidly turning dark grey, and the rain was flattening his hair and running down his face, he took two steps towards me and stopped. I noticed that Oscar made no move to go forward and greet him, preferring to hug the side of my van, where he got a little shelter from the torrential rain that was hammering down on the vehicles with a noise like thunder.

'Signor Armstrong, fancy meeting you here.' There was no warm welcome in his voice – very much the opposite. He looked and sounded decidedly menacing. As the rain soaked through his clothes and plastered his jacket against his body, I could clearly see the outline of a pistol in a holster under his left arm, and I instinctively took a step closer to my van.

He held up a hand and wagged his finger at me. 'You aren't going to go off and leave me, are you?' His voice hardened and I saw his right hand tense, ready to reach for the weapon. 'First, I need you to tell me what brings you here. Curiosity, maybe?'

By now, the rain had soaked right through my clothes and I could feel a small river running down my back, but that was the least of my worries. I rapidly considered my options – and there weren't many of them. If I tried to run, I knew he could shoot me down in seconds and there was something in his eyes that told me he wouldn't hesitate to kill yet another person. That look, every bit as much as the dried blood I'd just found, convinced me that I was standing in front of a serial killer. The death of a British private investigator would just add one more to his tally, and I felt sure he wouldn't bat an eyelid.

My brain was working overtime, desperately trying to come up with a way out of this predicament, as I did my best to stay positive, trying not to reflect on what might be going to happen to me. Flight was out of the question, so that left me with a choice of launching an attack or negotiating. Although I used to box for the Metropolitan Police in my younger days and I've always tried to keep myself pretty fit, I knew that I would have my work cut out against a fit, strong man many years my junior, even if I were to manage to get the gun off him in the first place. Shelving that option for now, I decided to try negotiation, and I did my best to produce a friendly smile.

'Inspector Faldo, what a coincidence. I often come here with Oscar for a walk.' An idea occurred to me. 'He's training to be a gun dog, ready to start retrieving waterfowl from the lake when the shooting season starts again. We've just come from there now.'

For a moment, I saw his expression relax but it didn't last long. 'Nice try, but we both know that's a lie, don't we? Whose idea was it to fill the cigar box with gravel? Was it yours or Pisano's?'

Any doubts I might have had about his guilt were swept away in an instant.

'Don't worry, though. I found the spy camera and I destroyed it.'

My mind registered that he had used the singular when referring to the camera so, if he were to kill me, hopefully, there would still be evidence in the other camera to prove that he'd been looking in the cigar box. This was, however, little comfort. For now, the more pressing thing on my mind was trying to come up with something that would prevent me from being killed. I tried pleading ignorance.

'Did you say a cigar box full of gravel? I don't understand.'

'Don't insult my intelligence, Armstrong. I know you were behind that.' His right hand moved a few inches closer to his open jacket and I tensed even more. 'So tell me, did somebody send in dashcam footage of my Land Rover or has Marco suddenly started remembering what happened?'

I knew that there was no point continuing to deny knowledge of what he'd done, so I tried a bit of bluff. 'Both, Faldo, since you ask. The door camera on the property directly opposite Marco's place has produced a beautifully clear image of the moment of impact when you tried to murder him. He still doesn't remember anything about the accident, thank God, but he remembers getting a phone call summoning him back to the office.'

I saw him shake his head in annoyance. 'I shouldn't have done that, but he was getting too close. I knew that sooner or later, he'd work it out. He had to be silenced, but how was I to know that being hit by a Land Rover wasn't going to kill him? I can't get to him now to finish the job so I have to get away. How annoying.' He made it sound as if it were Marco's fault. Certainly, there was no trace of pity or contrition in his voice. This guy was a psychopath. This realisation did little to slow my racing heart.

I kept my eyes trained on his right hand, fully prepared to launch myself at him if he reached for his weapon but knowing, deep down, that it would probably be a futile effort. We were about eight or ten feet apart, and by the time I reached him, the pistol would be in his hand. I remembered the message I'd left for Virgilio. I'd arrived here at the quarry at three and it was probably at least three-fifteen by now, maybe later. If he'd listened to my message as soon as he finished his tennis lesson, it was possible he could get himself here by half past three so, for now, all I could do was try to buy myself time by keeping Faldo talking. As he had freely admitted the attempted murder of Marco, I asked him about the diamonds.

'Tell me something, Faldo: how long have you been running the conflict-diamond operation at Santa Maria Novella station?' The rainwater was streaming down my face but I resisted the temptation to reach up and wipe my eyes, for fear that he might misinterpret the movement and pull out his gun. As long as that remained holstered, I had a fraction of a chance of survival.

His expression changed to one of considerable surprise. 'You know about that? How do you know about that?'

'Somebody I met told me. He's an asylum seeker and he sold some diamonds recently. Did he sell them to you, or do you have a go-between?' I stopped and then continued as if I'd just worked it out. 'Of course, you wouldn't dirty your hands, would you? It was Berg who collected the diamonds for you, wasn't it?'

To my surprise, he laughed. 'Berg collected the diamonds for *himself*. It was his little racket. I wasn't involved with him in the slightest. I only found out about him from an *extracomunitario* who was trying to sell some diamonds. I got him to tell me who the buyer was. It took me a month, but I managed to track that man down and he told me that he passed the diamonds on to a man called Berg on the Ponte Vecchio.'

'And so you killed all three of them.'

'Of course.' The matter-of-fact way he said it made my skin

creep. 'The two Africans were no loss to humanity, and the old man in the jewellery shop was a crook.'

Doing my best to keep the disgust out of my voice, I brought up the subject of the other murder. 'So why kill Jacobs? Did you think he had the diamonds?'

'Berg told me he'd sold them to Jacobs, but he didn't tell me that those diamonds were still in his own safe back home. What sort of imbecile pays three hundred thousand for a box of jewels and leaves them in the vendor's safe? I felt sure Jacobs must have had them, but then it turned out he didn't.'

'And when you found he didn't have them, you killed him.'

'What else could I do?' Once again, he was able to make it sound like the most normal thing in the world. He glanced around and I was bracing myself, about to launch myself at him, when he turned back again. A sinister smile appeared on his face. 'Go ahead and try, Armstrong; it won't do you any good. You're an old man now, and you know I can take you even without a gun.'

My ex-wife often said I was a strange character, and I have to admit that she probably had a point. In spite of the threat and the very real likelihood of my untimely demise, I found myself far more bothered by the fact that he had called me old, than by what might be about to happen to me. Considering that I'd just about run out of options, I decided to call his bluff.

I did my best to adopt a sneering tone. 'You, take me? I know old ladies who could beat you in a fair fight.'

That same manic smile appeared on his face. 'Yes, right, and you're one of those old ladies, I suppose.'

'Put your money where your mouth is. Drop the gun and let's fight it out as men.'

The sinister smile turned into an even more sinister laugh. '"Fight it out as men"? Just listen to yourself. This isn't a corny movie, Armstrong. No heroics for me. You're going to die and that's that. You see, I have no choice.'

'Why do you have no choice?' My eyes were fixed on his right hand, waiting for any sign of movement. My nerves and sinews were stretched to breaking point.

'You know too much, you see. It's your own fault. If you hadn't come snooping around here, you would never have seen me again. I'm off to pastures new.' He stopped and produced that same sinister laugh again. 'But it'll give me great satisfaction to settle accounts with you, you meddling fool. The moment I saw you here, I knew what I needed to do. You really shouldn't go sticking your nose into other people's business, you know.'

'What business would that be, Faldo? The diamond business or the psychotic serial-killer business?'

I saw him tense and a twitch appeared at the side of his mouth. I knew without a shadow of a doubt that he was going to kill me now, and my only hope was to get him so angry, he might make a mistake.

We stood there in silence for several seconds, the rain still pouring down and the tension between the two of us reaching as far as Oscar. Although I didn't take my eyes off Faldo's right hand for a second, I heard Oscar produce a rare growl. He could tell there was something wrong. Fortunately, Faldo also heard it and he shot a fearful sideways glance towards Oscar.

Taking advantage of Faldo's momentary lapse, I threw myself desperately towards him. His eyes turned back and his hand was already disappearing into his jacket when, wonderfully, help in the shape of a soaking-wet, black Labrador came to my rescue. Having sensed the tension in the air, Oscar launched himself towards Faldo, producing a totally out-of-character visceral snarl as he did so. This diverted Faldo's attention long enough for my outstretched arms to reach him and grab his right hand before he could draw the weapon. Even better, Faldo, seeing himself attacked on two fronts by two adversaries – one of whom was exhibiting a gleaming set of teeth – took a step backwards, slipped on the soaking-wet ground, and fell backwards into the mud with me on top of him.

His right hand was gripping the handle of the pistol that was halfway out of its holster while both of my hands desperately scrabbled for possession of the weapon. He landed heavily on his back, followed a split second later by my knee into his solar plexus with the full weight of my body behind it. I gave him a punch to the face, putting as much venom into the jab as possible, and had the satisfaction of seeing his head jerk backwards into the muddy ground. His body went limp for a moment and I was able to tear the pistol out of his grip without difficulty. Beside us, Oscar was growling fiercely but rather spoiling his performance by wagging his tail furiously as he did so. It looked as though he was having a wonderful time.

Faldo, on the other hand, appeared far more frightened of my normally docile pet Labrador than of the pistol now trained at his face. I glanced at the weapon and saw that it was a standard Beretta nine millimetre semi-automatic without a safety catch. Just so he could be under no misapprehension, I deliberately cocked it and held it closer to his face. As I did so, I heard a vehicle approaching and out of the corner of my eye, I glimpsed Virgilio's Alfa splashing through the puddles towards us. I didn't take my eyes off Faldo for a moment and I leant towards him.

'So who's the old lady now, Faldo? Here's the *commissario*. He's going to arrest you for multiple murders, and I hope you never see the light of day again.' I heard running feet approaching but I still kept my eyes on Faldo and the automatic pointed firmly at him.

'*Ciao*, Dan. I hope you realise you've made an awful mess of

Inspector Faldo's suit.' Virgilio's voice was heavy with irony. 'Oscar, get off. You're almost as muddy and wet as your master.' He came into my eyeline and I saw that he was also holding a pistol trained at the man on his back in the mud. 'Faldo, I want you to roll over onto your face and put your hands behind your back. If you want to make me a happy man, try putting up a fight. There's nothing I'd like more than to empty this pistol into you.' There was raw anger in his voice.

I knew how he felt.

22

___

THURSDAY AFTERNOON/EVENING

I went home for yet another change of clothes and found that Anna had come back from work and was waiting for me. Her reaction when she saw me was a mixture of relief and horror.

'Virgilio called Lina and she phoned to tell me what happened. You know you're crazy, don't you?'

I very nearly told her that I hadn't had a choice but then realised that I would have been copying the words of the psychopath we had just arrested. I could see Anna was worried so I did my best to play it down. 'Yes, pretty crazy considering I wasn't even being paid. Still, the shorts and the T-shirt will wash.'

'Why did you go there on your own? Would it have been too much trouble for you to phone the police and get them to come?'

I shook my head. 'I'm afraid it was more complicated than that. I'll tell you about it some time – or maybe I'll put it in my memoirs if I ever get around to writing them.'

'Lina told me Virgilio said you were very brave.' She was sounding less upset and more sympathetic now.

'Lina wasn't there. I was scared stiff, but sometimes you find yourself in the sort of position where all you can do is try to fight your way out of it.'

'Only *you* would have got yourself into that position in the first place. You could have been killed.' She reached towards me with both hands, realised what a soggy mess I was and made do with giving me a pat on the arm. 'I love you very dearly and I can't bear the thought of something happening to you.'

She was, of course, perfectly correct that I could have got myself killed but, once again, I did my best to play it down. I knew I would probably relive this afternoon's events in my dreams for many nights to come, but there was no point increasing her anxiety by telling her that if I hadn't tried to fight my way out of it, I felt sure I wouldn't be here now. Instead, I pointed to my bedraggled-looking dog – but I had no doubt that I looked just as drenched – and gave him the accolade he richly deserved.

'And I love you too, Anna, but it was okay, it was two against one. I had backup.' I squatted down on the kitchen floor and gave Oscar a well-deserved hug. I was still so wet that I barely felt his soggy fur against me. 'Thanks, old buddy, you're one heck of a wingman.'

In reply, he licked my cheek and then burrowed his head under my armpit, tail wagging cheerfully. I gave him a squeeze before standing up and holding out a hand towards Anna. 'I would give you a hug as well, *carissima*, but I'm still a bit damp.'

'A bit damp? You English and your love of understatement! Have you seen what you've done to the floor?'

My eyes followed the direction of her pointing hand and saw the mess Oscar and I had made. There were actual puddles on the terracotta. I glanced back at her. 'If you think that's bad, you should see the inside of the van. Sorry about that. I think I'd better go and change, hadn't I?'

She gave an exasperated sigh, softened by the smile on her

face. 'And I get the pleasure of drying this soggy beast out, I suppose?'

Oscar chose to ignore the 'soggy beast' comment and wandered across to lean heavily against her leg, looking up at her with soulful eyes. She reached down to ruffle his ears before returning her attention to me. 'You might just as well leave all your clothes down here and I'll throw them in the washing machine along with a pair of trousers that I found in the bathroom with a massive coffee stain on them and which are now soaking in a bucket.'

Obediently, I removed my trainers, which were still half full of water, peeled off my wet clothes, and went upstairs to shower and change.

By the time I came back downstairs again, I was feeling a whole lot better, although the knuckles of my right hand were giving me a bit of grief from where I'd punched Faldo. Still, I told myself, it had been worth it and I would happily do it again to a monster like him. Downstairs, the kitchen smelled of damp dog, although the hero of the hour was standing shivering with his tail between his legs while Anna ran the hair-dryer over him. He's a brave dog in important situations, but hair-dryers and vacuum cleaners terrify him.

Anna looked up when she saw me and nodded approvingly. To Oscar's relief, she turned off the hair-dryer and stood up. He immediately shook himself and started rolling about on the now dry kitchen floor, all four legs in the air, tail wagging happily now that the noisy implement of torture had gone away. Clearly our close call earlier this afternoon hadn't worried him in the slightest. As for me, I was just happy to be alive and I went over to give Anna a warm hug and a kiss. She gripped my arms with both her hands and looked up at me.

'I'm very proud of you, Dan, but you frighten the life out of me on occasions.' She added a kiss of her own to soften her words.

'I frighten the life out of myself on occasions but, in this case, I had no alternative. I wish I could explain it to you, but until I get the all-clear from Virgilio, I can't say a word about it.'

At that moment, my phone – which had justified the maker's claim that it was water-resistant – started ringing. I disentangled myself from Anna, picked it up, and was delighted to see that it was none other than Marco Innocenti.

'*Ciao*, Marco. Am I glad to hear from you! How are you? I would have come to see you, but I was told they were limiting visitors.'

'*Ciao*, Dan.' I was delighted to hear his voice sounding near enough normal and, in fact, quite excited. It soon turned out there was a reason for this. 'I've just been speaking to the *commissario*, and he's told me what happened at the quarry. I actually called *him* at three to tell him that my memory's been steadily coming back to me and I'd just remembered that it was Faldo who called me that afternoon, ordering me back to the station in a hurry. Faldo said something bad had happened to the *commissario*, and he needed me pronto. Thanks for catching that maniac, Dan. We owe you.'

'Oscar did most of the work, but I did have the satisfaction of punching Faldo in the face. He was a really unpleasant piece of work. I'm just glad he's behind bars now.'

'The *commissario* told me to ask you if you could call him. He's in his office.'

'I'll do that right away. I'm delighted to hear you sounding all right again. You had us worried for a few moments.'

He laughed. 'The *commissario* said he wasn't worried. He says my head's too thick and solid.'

I laughed in return. 'Take it from me, he was as nervous as

hell – we all were. How long before you're going to be back on the beat?'

'Another three days lying on my back and then they're going to start physiotherapy. They say I should be upright again within a week and I'll come back to work as soon as the medics tell me it's all right.'

I wished him well and immediately called Virgilio as requested. He, too, was sounding animated when he answered.

'*Ciao*, Dan. How are you feeling?'

'Dry again, thank God. I'm just going to have a cup of coffee and then I'll come down to the office so we can check the footage from the camera that survived the intervention by our friend Faldo.'

'You'll do no such thing. You take it easy. We've got him now. It can wait until tomorrow.' I heard him chuckle. 'Besides, haven't you got to learn your lines?'

My heart sank. 'Ah, you know about that, do you?'

'Anna told Lina and she told me. She's booked us tickets for Saturday night.'

'That's all I need! I've been hoping to keep my appearance low-key – I'm only doing it because I was badgered into it, you know.'

I could still hear the mirth in his voice. 'And I've spread the word around the *questura*. There should be quite a crowd to see you strutting your stuff.'

'I don't know whether to thank you or come down there and thump you. And I will come down there now. I've got a couple of pieces of evidence I managed to get off the front of Faldo's Land Rover and they need to go to Forensics.' I checked my watch and saw that, remarkably, it wasn't even four-thirty yet. So much had happened in the last hour. 'I'll be with you by five-thirty.'

I left Oscar snacking on biscuits with Anna and drove down

to the *questura* perched on two folded beach towels and a plastic bag. The driver's seat was absolutely soaked through and the carpet at my feet like a swamp. To make matters worse, I could barely see out of the back window after Oscar had shaken himself enthusiastically on our way back from the quarry, liberally coating the inside of the windows with a mixture of mud and malodorous 'Eau de Labrador'. The good news was that the rain had stopped as suddenly as it had started, and I was able to complete the journey with the windows open, so that I was able to arrive at the police station smelling a good bit better than I would have done otherwise.

I found Virgilio in his tennis clothes, which were probably a whole lot drier than what he'd been wearing at the quarry. He jumped to his feet as I walked in and came over to give me a bear hug. 'Dan, Dan, what would we do without you? You could have got yourself killed, you know.'

I gave him a smile and pushed him off me. 'So Anna keeps telling me. To be honest, I only went to the quarry to look for evidence. I wasn't trying to be anybody's hero. You were out of contact, and I thought about calling for backup, but, with everybody here being under suspicion, the only person I could have called is the *questore* and I don't have his direct number. Where's Faldo?'

'Safely locked up in a cell downstairs, changed into prison uniform in place of his wet clothes.' He smiled. 'The convict clothes suit him, which is just as well as he's hopefully going to be wearing them for the rest of his life.'

'Did he tell you why he chose to come out to the quarry at that particular moment?'

'He told me he was tidying up a few odds and ends before leaving. Those are the exact words he used – as if he were just doing a few little jobs around the place. With Marco still alive, he knew we would soon be onto him, so he booked himself onto a flight from Rome to Johannesburg tomorrow morning. Interestingly, the booking was just for him, not his wife or kids. He was only interested in covering his own back.' He went back to his chair and sat down. 'It's amazing how you can work with somebody for months, years, without realising that you're working with a madman. Thank God you stopped him when you did. Who knows how many other people he would have killed if he'd managed to get away and start a new life?'

Johannesburg stirred a memory in me. 'I noticed on social media that he and his family went to South Africa on holiday a year or two ago. Maybe that's where he heard about conflict diamonds being smuggled into Europe by asylum seekers. Anyway, shall we take a look at the camera footage of the cigar box?'

I checked the app on my phone and, sure enough, there was Inspector Roberto Faldo levering open Virgilio's desk drawer and removing the box from the evidence bag. The expression on his face when he discovered that the contents weren't diamonds after all was a picture. In a matter of a very few seconds, we could clearly see realisation dawn on him that he'd been caught in a trap. We saw him hastily drop the cigar box back into the drawer and search the office desperately until he found the other camera and then make a run for it.

I looked up and caught Virgilio's eye. 'With Marco's confirmation that it was Faldo who made the phone call on Wednesday afternoon and this video, you should easily be able to make the attempted murder charge stick against him. Hopefully, you'll also see his Land Rover on the video footage of the vehicles in the area around the time of the hit.' I reached into my pocket and brought out the two rolled-up poo bags, one containing the bloodstained plastic from the Land Rover's light and the other containing the piece of material from Marco's trousers. 'Here, these should also help. I peeled them off the front of the Land Rover just before the rain started. Forensics should be able to get Marco's DNA off the dried blood on the light. And don't forget that Faldo told me everything and I'll be delighted to give evidence against him.'

Virgilio took the bags from me. 'Thanks, again, Dan. We can certainly nail him for the attempted murder of Marco, and, with your evidence, we should also be able to pin Jacobs's murder on him and the others as well. I've been in touch with the Grand Hotel and they've sent me the CCTV footage from the dining-room cameras – which Faldo deliberately omitted to mention. Who do we see sitting there, eating his way happily through a hundred-euro meal, but Faldo? He looks as if he hasn't a care in the world when he gets up at ten-fifteen and heads off with a bag in his hands – no doubt containing the hoodie – to commit murder. Mind you, he wasn't holding back in the car on his way here. It was almost as if he was proud of what he'd done. He's singing like a canary.'

'I hope he continues to do so. Have you given the Berg family the good news that you've nailed the killer? Presumably, they'll be off back to the Netherlands.' A thought occurred to me. 'What about Axel Jacobs's diamonds? Have you been able to contact his next of kin?'

'Yes, his daughter and her husband have been informed. He's in the oil industry and they live in Dallas, Texas. As far as I can tell, there's been little or no contact between her and her father for many years. When I told her he'd brought three hundred thousand euros' worth of gold bars to pay for conflict diamonds, which were going to be held as evidence in the murder case, the woman didn't sound in the least upset. She told me she had no interest in either her father or his "dirty money" – those are the words she used – and she told me she would be more than happy for anything of his to go to charity. That saves me a lot of paper-work and saves the courts a lot of time, but it's sad all the same that neither of these two old men will be missed by their children.'

I nodded in agreement. 'Maybe it's like the Scottish professor told me: blood diamonds are called that for a reason. They corrupt everyone they touch. I've been wondering why David Berg contacted me last Friday night. He was clearly worried about something. I suppose it was because he'd found out that his contact at the station had been murdered, and he was afraid he would be next. Presumably, because he was involved with the illegal diamond trade, he felt he couldn't come straight to the police.'

Virgilio got to his feet. 'I'm sure you're right. It's a pity for him that he chose to get involved with such a dirty business. And now, if you have time, the *questore* has asked us both to go up and see him.'

I followed him up to the top floor, where we were ushered into the *questore*'s office by his secretary. As soon as he saw us, he leapt nimbly to his feet and came across to pump my hand vigor-ously up and down.

'Signor Armstrong, I wanted to shake your hand and thank you in person for your outstanding bravery in bringing a truly evil man to justice.'

I repeated my usual line about having gone to the quarry simply to look for evidence and not having done anything partic-ularly heroic, but he was having none of it.

'I'm going to put your name forward for a gallantry award. Excellent, excellent. Thank the Lord that we no longer have a traitor in our midst, and not only a traitor but a sadistic serial killer as well.'

He asked if there was any more practical way he could reward me, and Virgilio was quick to step in and tell him about the spy camera that Faldo had smashed. The *questore* nodded enthusiastically. 'Of course, of course, buy Signor Armstrong a new one – no, get him two of them.'

By the time I left his office, I'd been told I was going to receive not only two new cameras but also several cases of expensive Villa Antinori wine and a new suit, made to measure by the *questore*'s own personal tailor with his compliments. This, of course, meant that I would now have two brand-new suits and very little opportunity to wear either of them. Still, I told myself, it's the thought that counts.

As Virgilio walked me back down the stairs, he added one more bonus. 'You and Anna – and Oscar, of course – will be the guests of the Florence police for a slap-up dinner after Saturday night's show.'

23

SATURDAY EVENING

By the time I got to the Teatro dell'Arno on Saturday night, I was a nervous wreck. Anna drove us there while I sat in the passenger seat and had a last run-through of my lines. Friday's final dress rehearsal hadn't gone too badly – apart from a wardrobe malfunction when a seam of my character's grubby overalls gave way, revealing me in an old pair of Marks & Spencer boxer shorts – and I had more or less managed to produce the right lines at the right moments. Monica and Tiberio had been very supportive and he'd even helped me stick a crib sheet onto the side of the cupboard against which I spent much of the first act leaning, looking moody.

In spite of what Zebra had said, the plot definitely had Shakespearean undertones. The main characters were involved in an ill-fated love affair complicated by the fact that Monica's uncle, my character, and her father were members of the fascist party, while the love of her life, Tiberio's character, was involved with the local resistance movement. The tragic denouement – reminiscent of *Romeo and Juliet* – resulted in the deaths of both of the young people, causing the characters around them to reassess all their beliefs. I had to hand it to Zebra; not only was she an excellent director, but she had also written a powerful play, and if all went well I was convinced that the audience would enjoy it.

Anna kissed me and wished me luck when we reached the stage door before she led Oscar around to the main entrance and the seats reserved for the two of them. Zebra had been most insistent that Oscar should be invited and when I first walked out onto the stage, I could see him lounging comfortably in the front row like a theatre habitué.

The first act passed in a flash and when I joined the other actors in the common room during the interval, I was only too happy to gulp down a cold beer from the fridge. Zebra came in to give us a team talk and I was reminded of similar pep talks I'd received back in my rugby-playing days – although her language was a lot less colourful than those had often been. Her clothes made up for any lack of colour in her speech. Tonight, she was dressed from head to toe in a long and voluminous yellow and black gown that reminded me of Amy Mackintosh and her hen-party tiger costume.

I actually began to enjoy myself during the second act, which was ironic because the story was becoming increasingly tense until the violent and tragic ending. When the curtains finally came down – or, rather, were dragged jerkily into the centre of the stage from the sides – the audience erupted into applause that sounded quite genuine. Monica and Tiberio went out into the limelight to another roar of applause and were joined by Zebra. The curtains were then dragged open again and the rest of the actors, me included, walked out and took a bow to more applause.

When the lights came on in the auditorium, I was delighted to see the mayor applauding enthusiastically, and Virgilio on his feet only a few rows behind him, clapping and whistling. As for

Oscar, he looked mildly surprised by all the noise, but was clearly far too comfortable to think about joining the standing ovation.

I changed quickly and went out to the lobby that had been transformed into a bar. Out here I found, not only Virgilio and Lina, but also no lesser a personage than Giuseppe Verdi, the *vice questore*, accompanied by a woman half his age. I decided to give him the benefit of the doubt and told myself that she could be his niece – not that I really believed that. He caught my eye for a moment, no doubt registering that I was the man with the Labrador who had been in Virgilio's office, but he had the good manners to clap his hands together and mouth, '*Bravo*' at me. Oscar was with Anna and he had by this time worked out that waitresses – Amélie and Vanda – were circulating with trays of nibbles and he immediately adopted his *they don't feed me, I'm wasting away* expression that won him quite a few tasty titbits.

I introduced Anna to Zebra, who immediately kissed her and told her at great length how lucky she was to be partnered with a wonderful man like me. I caught Anna's eye and winked – she knows me far too well by now to be taken in by that. Zebra then went on to give us the good news that her friend, the former theatrical agent, had been in the audience and had been blown away by Monica's performance. As a result, he had promised to arrange an interview for her with a well-known agent in Rome, which might lead to greater things. I was happy for her and I wondered how this might affect her relationship with Tiberio.

As Zebra went off to schmooze more guests, I noticed the mayor standing on the far side of the room and when he spotted me, he waved us over. I introduced Anna and he introduced us to his wife – they were both looking very happy and very proud, and quite rightly so. We chatted briefly before Monica herself appeared and received hugs and kisses from her parents. She was bubbling with excitement after having had a talk with Zebra's agent friend. As we had expected, she hadn't brought Tiberio with her to meet her parents, but that was soon rectified. The mayor spotted a tall, grey-haired man across the room and beckoned to him and his wife to come over. They did so, and along with them came Tiberio.

The mayor shook hands with his political opponent and then introduced us to Umberto Carbone and his wife and made a point of going up to Tiberio and shaking his hand warmly. 'Congratulations on an outstanding performance. You must be my good friend Umberto's boy. The last time I saw you, you were about ten.'

I distinctly saw Tiberio catch Monica's eye and I read surprise on both their faces before Monica followed her father across to Tiberio and grabbed hold of his arm with both her hands. 'Papa, I'd like you to meet my boyfriend, Tiberio.'

I took Anna's arm and led her away so that the two families could bond without being disturbed. Virgilio and Lina were standing by the bar and he had two glasses of beer in his hands, one of which he held out towards me.

'*Ciao*, Dan, you can have them both if you like. I imagine you're ready for a drink before I drag you away for dinner.'

Lina came over and kissed me on the cheek. 'Well, that's a side of you I never expected to see. Who would have thought you were an actor?'

Anna clearly felt she had to set the record straight. 'To be honest, Lina, he's a very talented actor. He spends most of his life giving quite a convincing performance of being a sensible adult, but we all know that underneath the veneer, he's just a crazy fool.' She reached up and kissed me. 'But he's my crazy fool.'

A movement at my feet made me glance down and I intercepted a look from Oscar that clearly indicated that he felt that his relationship with me should also be recognised. I bent down and ruffled his ears.

'But there's nothing foolish about you, Oscar. I don't know what I'd do without you.'

He wagged his tail and, for a moment, it looked as though he winked at me.

* * *

MORE FROM T. A. WILLIAMS

In case you missed it, the previous instalment in the Armstrong and Oscar cozy mystery series from T. A. Williams, *Murder in the Tuscan Hills*, is available to order now here:

www.mybook.to/MurderintheTuscanHills

ACKNOWLEDGEMENTS

Warmest thanks to Emily Ruston, my lovely editor at the marvellous Boldwood Books, as well as the rest of the Boldwood team. Sincere thanks also to Sue Smith and Emily Reader for picking up all my errors and making sure that everything makes sense. Special thanks to the talented Simon Mattacks for producing the audio versions of all the books in the Dan and Oscar series. To me, he sounds just as Dan should sound. Finally, thanks to Mariangela, my wife, whose encyclopaedic knowledge of Italian history and culture never ceases to amaze me.

ABOUT THE AUTHOR

T. A. Williams is the author of The Armstrong and Oscar Cozy Mystery Series, cosy crime stories set in his beloved Italy, featuring the adventures of DCI Armstrong and his labrador Oscar. Trevor lives in Devon with his Italian wife.

Sign up to T. A. Williams' newsletter to read an EXCLUSIVE short story!

Visit T. A. Williams' website: www.tawilliamsbooks.com

Follow T. A. Williams' on social media:

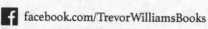

facebook.com/TrevorWilliamsBooks

x.com/TAWilliamsBooks

bsky.app/profile/tawilliamsbooks.bsky.social

ALSO BY T. A. WILLIAMS

Poison
& Pens

POISON & PENS IS THE HOME OF
COZY MYSTERIES SO POUR YOURSELF
A CUP OF TEA & GET SLEUTHING!

DISCOVER PAGE-TURNING NOVELS FROM
YOUR FAVOURITE AUTHORS &
MEET NEW FRIENDS

JOIN OUR
FACEBOOK GROUP

BIT.LYPOISONANDPENSFB

SIGN UP TO OUR
NEWSLETTER

BIT.LY/POISONANDPENSNEWS

Boldwood

Boldwood Books is an award-winning fiction publishing company seeking out the best stories from around the world.

Find out more at www.boldwoodbooks.com

Join our reader community for brilliant books, competitions and offers!

Follow us
@BoldwoodBooks
@TheBoldBookClub

Sign up to our weekly deals newsletter

https://bit.ly/BoldwoodBNewsletter

www.ingramcontent.com/pod-product-compliance
Lightning Source LLC
Chambersburg PA
CBHW012135040525
26165CB00015B/1059